A Happy Christmas

TONY WHELPTON

Published in 2016 by FeedARead.com Publishing

Copyright © Tony Whelpton

Cover image: Santa Claus with the kids © andresr

A CIP catalogue record for this title is available from the British Library.

*To my grandchildren and great-grandchildren,
who give me so much joy*

Other novels by Tony Whelpton

Before the Swallow Dares

The Heat of the Kitchen

Billy's War

There's No Pride In Prejudice
(Sequel to *Billy's War*)

All these books are available as e-books and as
paperbacks, some in hardbacks as well.
For details see either Tony's website
www.literarylounge.co.uk
or whichever Amazon site you normally use.

Chapter One
Nottingham 1986

Wilf Broadhurst was an unhappy man, a very unhappy man. In fact much more than that, he was not only a desperately unhappy but also a very lonely man.

In a literal sense, his loneliness could in no way be described as being of long standing; in fact he had been living alone for a little more than a year, for it was only thirteen months since his wife Cissy had died.

But the real solitude he felt was internal, deep within himself, and that, along with his unhappiness, whilst it had undoubtedly been aggravated by Cissy's death, went back much further: its roots stretched back nearly thirty years. In one sense Cissy had been the cause of his unhappiness, albeit a reluctant cause, and Wilf, for his part, would have been unwilling to impute blame to her; he preferred to believe – and it was indeed an entirely plausible explanation – that what had transpired had been the result of nothing more than a misunderstanding. But what a catastrophic misunderstanding!

Wilf was born in 1912 at 5 Wallan Street, in the Radford district of Nottingham, and he was the victim of tragedy very early in his life, for his father was one of the first casualties of the curiously-named *Great War*, and Wilf, or to give him his full name Wilfred James, never really knew his Dad, for he was not quite two years old by the time his father went to war. Nor was that the only way in which his family life was disrupted during his early years, for he was brought up partly by Dolly, his Mam, and partly by Dolly's own mother, because, as a young war-widow, Dolly would have been totally unable to survive – let alone look after her little son – if she had not gone to work in the nearby tobacco factory. Even so the young Wilf thrived. He was fit, he was intelligent; by comparison with most of the pupils at the Elementary School he attended, he was genuinely interested in learning. He left school at fourteen, however, even though it was clear to his teachers that he would have been capable of pursuing his studies further, because boys of his class and background simply did not stay on at school; in the factory where he went to work he was regarded by everyone as one of the brightest, and, by the factory girls, as one of the most handsome.

In 1935, when he was already twenty-three, he started going out with Cissy. She was by no means his first girlfriend, but she was the only one so far with whom he might find it remotely possible to share his life. Cissy's real name was Cecilia, but at a very early stage in her life she decided that name was too pretentious – 'too posh' was how she put it herself, and she chose to be called Cissy instead; in fact very few of her friends ever discovered that she had originally been christened Cecilia. Cissy too lived in Radford, and, like Wilf, she worked in one of the huge Player's cigarette factories which dominated the area. Even if you had walked through the district with your eyes shut you would have been able to discern that you were near a cigarette factory, for the whole area reeked of tobacco; not from the smell of stale cigarette smoke which in those days characterised the local public bars, but from the sweet, heady – and initially, at least, not unpleasant – odour of the freshly cured tobacco from which the cigarettes were made. What was more, it was an odour which clung to the clothes and the persons of those who worked there, to the point where even a bath, a shampoo and a change of clothes on returning home was not sufficient to conceal the identity of your workplace from your companions on an evening out.

Two years later, just a few days after the Coronation of the present Queen's father, King George VI, Wilf and Cissy married, and in the following year Cissy gave birth to a daughter, whom they named Susan. But – just like his own father – Wilf had little time in which to get properly acquainted with his little daughter, for of course, along with most men of his age, he was conscripted into the army in September 1939, right at the very beginning of World War II; in consequence he was absent throughout her formative years, for she was already nearly eight years old when Wilf was eventually allowed to leave the army in the autumn of 1946. Sadly, during the years when, ideally, he should have been at home getting to know his new daughter, he had been otherwise occupied at places like Dunkirk, Benghazi, Tobruk, Tripoli, Monte Cassino, Berlin... But at least, he comforted himself, he had ultimately returned home; many thousands had not.

In common with many returning soldiers, he found it hard to settle back into civilian life, hard even to rekindle the loving friendship which he had enjoyed with Cissy in the early months of their marriage. During the six years of his absence Cissy had established a routine in which no one other than she herself and her daughter mattered; as long as she provided Susan with regular meals, there was nobody else to take into consideration: she could eat what she liked and when she liked, go to bed when she liked, and, when her mother was willing to come over and baby-sit, go out when she liked and also with whom she liked – but never alone with a man, for she maintained a strict adherence to traditional values as she understood them, especially her marriage vows.

Initially, of course, their 1946 reunion was joyful, but before long it became clear to her that Wilf, like many ex-servicemen, had become more introvert during his time in the army; he would sit for hours on end staring into the fire and saying nothing. Paradoxically, however, he could also be more demanding, especially where the timing of meals was concerned; in particular they had frequent arguments when Cissy wanted to go out with the friends who had been her lifeline during her lonely wartime years.

His relationship with his daughter was not especially happy either, for when he returned from the war he was a total stranger to her, and he often found her habits and her demands irritating. When she entered her teens it was even worse; because he had not been there to lay the foundations of a sound relationship in the early years of her life, Susan resented what she regarded as his 'bossy' attitude, although, in truth, he was no more authoritarian than most fathers of his generation.

Wilf and Cissy's marriage could not, therefore, be described as being of the happiest imaginable, even if they had no fights worthy of the name. Essentially they just accepted their marriage as an unalterable fact, and settled into a routine where there was little excitement and no romance, a fact which, however, did little or nothing to assuage Wilf's grief when Cissy died.

Tony Whelpton

Chapter Two
Nottingham 1958

'More tea, Wilf?'

'No thanks, Cissy, that's enough for me.'

'What about you, Sue? Another cup?'

'No.'

'No what?'

'No tea.'

'That's not what I meant! I'll try again then. More tea?'

Susan looked in an exasperated fashion at her mother, then answered sarcastically, 'Thank you, mother, no thank you. I don't want any more tea, mother, but thank you for asking.'

'You saucy young madam!' Cissy exclaimed.

'What's up now?' Susan retorted. 'I said thank you! Or was it something else that was getting on your nerves?'

'I'll give you a good hiding if you don't watch out, big as you are!' said her mother angrily.

'You and whose army?'

'Hey! Give over!' Wilf ordered, looking up momentarily from the *Nottingham Evening Post* which had been commanding his attention throughout tea.

'A fat lot of help you are!' Cissy grumbled. 'I've done my best to teach her some manners, but what chance do I stand when you sit reading the paper all through every meal we have?'

Observing that her mother's temper had now been diverted towards her father, Susan got up from the tea table and was about to leave the room.

'And where do you think you're going?' Cissy demanded.

'Oh, I'm sorry, mama! Please forgive me, mama! Please may I leave the table, mama?'

'Don't you get all lah-de-dah with me, you little hussy!'

'Sorry! I thought that's what you wanted,' Susan snapped. 'I don't know why you can't make your mind up! One minute you want me to be polite, and the next minute you don't like it if I am!'

With that Susan left the room, slamming the door behind her – in fact, during Susan's teenage years, the slamming of doors was one of the most frequent sounds to be heard in the Broadhurst household. Her mother vainly tried to enlist her husband's support, but ultimately the pages of the *Nottingham Evening Post* proved a greater attraction than her attempt to launch a good manners offensive. Heaving a deep sigh, Cissy proceeded to clear the tea table and take the dishes into the scullery.

Ten minutes later, with the washing-up done, she returned to the kitchen, as the living-room was habitually called in Nottingham, at least in their stratum of society, even though it was virtually never used for the preparation of food; seeing Wilf still engrossed by the evening paper she sighed, picked up her knitting and a copy of *Woman's Weekly,* and retreated into her own world, only to be dragged back to reality when the kitchen door opened and Susan reappeared.

'I'm off out,' she said. 'Don't wait up – I may be late.'

'Where are you off to then?' asked her father without looking up from his paper.

'I'm just going down to the *Chase,*' she replied.

At last Wilf looked up. 'You're going where?'

'I'm going to the *Chase Tavern,* I told you.'

'What!'

'It's a pub, Dad.'

'Yes, I know very well what it is, and I don't like it. You're too young to be going out drinking.'

'I'm nineteen…'

'Yes, and that's too young for a girl to go pub-crawling on her own, isn't it, Cissy?'

'Yes, it is – and just look at you! Your mouth's smothered with lipstick, and what on earth have you done to your eyes?'

'Oh mother, for God's sake, it's eye shadow!'

'Well, it looks a mess, and don't blaspheme! And yes, your Dad's right, you are too young to be going into pubs on your own!'

'Well, I'm not going to be on my own, so that's all right, isn't it!'

13

Susan made for the door, but Cissy was not yet finished.

'So who are you going to the pub with?'

'A friend.'

'Which friend?'

'Nobody you know.'

'What's her name?'

'Courtney.'

'Courtney? What sort of name's that for a girl?' asked Wilf.

'Courtney's not a girl.'

'What!' Susan's mother exploded. 'When did you start going to pubs with men?'

'I'm not going to pubs, and I'm not going with men either,' Susan insisted. 'I'm going to one pub, and I'm going with one man. His name's Courtney, and he's a very respectable young man.'

'How old is he?' asked her father.

'Where does he come from?' asked her mother almost simultaneously.

'He's the same age as me, and he lives in St Ann's the same as we do, but he originally came from Jamaica,' replied Susan, 'and we've been going out for six weeks and I haven't failed to come home yet, have I?'

Before her shocked parents had time to react, Susan had left the house, slamming first the kitchen door and then the front door behind her.

It was a Saturday evening shortly before the end of August 1958, and the Broadhurst family were at home, home now being a terraced house in Bluebell Hill Road in the St Ann's district of Nottingham. They had moved there shortly after the birth of Susan, when Wilf had changed jobs, working now in the factory of the Boots Pure Drug Company in Island Street, which was within walking distance of Bluebell Hill Road. Unlike many soldiers returning to civilian life in 1945 and 1946, Wilf had been fortunate enough to be able to return to his old job; the Boots factory itself was not particularly pleasant to work in, because of the stench given off by the manufacturing processes involved, but at least, unlike the tobacco factories, its effects were only detectable in the immediate vicinity of the factory site, and certainly not as far away as Bluebell Hill Road.

In actual fact the name of the road in which they lived was something of a misnomer in every respect: it was indeed a road, and part of the road involved a fairly steep hill, but if there had ever been any bluebells to be seen on the hill after which the road was named, it must have been many years ago, for the houses had been built towards the end of the nineteenth century, and virtually all of them were now in a state of disrepair, for they were rented, not owner-occupied, and the vast majority of the owners were not in the habit of repairing defects in properties from which they derived such little income.

In this respect Bluebell Hill Road was no different from any other road in the neighbourhood; if anything it was in better shape than most. Almost all the houses in St Ann's were terraced houses, with no interior bathrooms or toilets, and there were ten thousand of them; there was a public bath house in St Ann's Well Road, and that was well used, but for the vast majority of the inhabitants bath night involving bringing in a metal bath-tub, which was normally to be found hanging on a nail affixed to the outside wall of the toilet which stood in the back yard, and filling it with water heated in the coal-fired copper situated in one corner of the scullery. It was habitual for every member of a family to take it in turns to use the water, for the copper was only big enough to heat the water to fill one bath-tub, but, in any case, very few of them would have been able to afford the coal necessary to heat the water they would need if everyone were to have clean water to bathe in. A large area of St Ann's had been scheduled for slum clearance and subsequent redevelopment well before the war, but, like many such schemes throughout the country, this was put on hold for a considerable period of time, and now that the city had witnessed a large influx of immigrants from both the West Indies and the Indian sub-continent, this was one of the few areas where those immigrants could afford to settle. In consequence the scheduled redevelopment was postponed yet again.

'Why didn't you stop her going out like that?' demanded Cissy.

'When have either of us been able to stop her doing anything she wanted to do?' Wilf countered.

'It's your fault – you should have put your foot down a long time ago!'

'If I'd been here, I would have done! But I was away fighting for King and Country, wasn't I! You were the only one looking after her at the time it mattered, so it's got to be your fault, not mine!'

'I had enough to do as it was! You always try to put the blame on me. What do you think it was like for me, having to do everything myself?'

'I know it was hard for you, but it was hard for everybody during the war, wasn't it! But some people still managed to bring up kids without them becoming snotty little brats!'

'You don't know what you're talking about! So tell me, when did you get back from the war? 1946, wasn't it? And what year is it now? 1958! That's twelve years since you've been back, so don't you go putting all the blame on me! She didn't start going out to pubs when she was six, did she!'

'Well, I never took her to a pub!'

'Neither did I! And look at her now – she's going out to a pub with a black man!'

'How do you know he's black?'

'It stands to reason – he's called Courtney, and he comes from Jamaica.'

'I expect there are some white people in Jamaica…'

'How many do you know?'

'I don't know anybody from Jamaica, white or black.'

'All right, so tell me this – suppose he is black, what are you going to do about it?'

'What do you want me to do – paint him white?'

'Don't be daft! You know what I mean – what will you do if he is?'

'Nothing.'

'Nothing? Are you happy about her going out with a black man?'

'Not particularly – but it depends what he's like.'

'We know what he's like. He's black.'

'Well, I'm sure there must be some that are nice…'

'I don't care whether he's nice or not! Do you want your daughter marrying a black?'

'Oh, I didn't know they were thinking of getting married…'

'I reckon she'll have to!'

'Why?'

'She'll go and get herself in the family way, you mark my words! And I'm not having any daughter of mine getting in that state and not being wed!'

'You're jumping to conclusions, you are! What makes you think she'll do that?'

'Well, if she's going out with a black man, Lord knows what they'll get up to!'

'I didn't know the colour of the man's skin had anything to do with it! Look at Lily's girl next door but one – she got herself into trouble, and the man she went with wasn't black!'

'That's different – Lily's girl's a little slut! Our Sue's not like that…'

'I know, and that's what I think too. So how could she get herself pregnant? It takes two, doesn't it?'

'Huh! Or one man that's like an animal…'

'Have you seen this bloke that our Sue's going out with?'

'No, and I don't want to either!'

'So how do you know he's like an animal?'

'Of course he is – he's black, isn't he?'

'I still don't know how you can say that if you haven't even met him!'

'I don't want to meet him either…'

'You might have to. What if you heard a knock at the door one day and when you went to see who it was you found it was him? What would you say to him?'

'I'd tell him to get out.'

'Politely?'

'Don't be daft – no, of course not!'

'And you'd say that, even without finding out if the man your daughter was keen on was a nice bloke or not? That's really nice, that is! I wonder what he'd say to our Sue about her Mam after that…'

'I don't care. It's just not right.'

The argument continued for a further twenty minutes without moving forward an inch, and only finished when Cissy went to fetch herself a new ball of wool for her knitting, while Wilf buried himself once more in the *Evening Post*.

Meanwhile, as it was a fairly warm summer's evening – and also because neither of them had enough money to spend a great deal of time drinking in the pub, Susan and Courtney went for a walk along Robin Hood Chase. Although it was not actually a park, Robin Hood Chase was the nearest thing to a park in that neighbourhood – at least there were trees and grass lining the path and no cars or buses were allowed, and it stretched over a mile from St Ann's Well Road at one end to Woodborough Road at the other. They walked slowly, chatting happily, stopping to exchange a word now and then with a few of the many children who were playing there; Courtney in particular enjoyed talking to young children. He was the eldest child of a large family, most of whom had remained in Jamaica whilst he and his father had come to Britain because there were no jobs to be had at home but insufficient workers in Britain, in some occupations at any rate, and he missed playing with his little brothers and sisters more than anything else – which was one of his characteristics that Susan most admired.

They walked roughly half a mile and then turned back, feeling that to walk the length of Robin Hood's Chase would take them too long, at least if they maintained the leisurely pace they had kept so far, for it had taken them almost an hour to reach that point, and at that speed they would not have been able to get back to the pub before closing time.

In fact their progress was a little speedier on the return leg, largely because most of the little children they had stopped to talk to had now gone home, and so, about half an hour later, they arrived at the *Chase Tavern*. Courtney opened the door leading to the Public Bar and held it open for Susan. The bar was crowded, as it always was on a Saturday evening, and there were no seats to be had; there was nothing unusual about that, for the benches affixed to the wall tended to fill up at an early stage in the evening and rarely became available again. There were very few free-standing chairs; if patrons wanted seats of that nature they would need to go into the Lounge, but comparatively few did, for the beer was more expensive in the Lounge than in the Public Bar, and times were hard: the boom of the early 50s which had prompted Prime Minister Harold Macmillan to proclaim only the previous year, 'You've never had it so good', was already over. In one corner of the bar a middle-aged man was playing the piano, an instrument so out of tune that it was almost impossible to recognise most of the songs he was playing, which did not prevent the majority of the customers singing along; for most of them the amount of beer they had already consumed was sufficient for them to be totally unaware of their lack of musicality or, alternatively, for them not to care. In another corner there was a group of older men seated around a table playing cribbage and drinking, smoking and singing as they played. In one of the remaining corners were the earnest darts players, oblivious to everyone else and, indeed, to everything but their game – except on those occasions when the point of a dart struck a wire on the board and ricocheted perilously close to another group of young men who occupied the fourth corner and who had already consumed more beer than was good for them, and who reacted belligerently, especially when it happened three times in rapid succession.

Among this group Susan noticed a boy whom she knew and whom she had been out with a few times before she met Courtney, but she chose to ignore him as they went past. At the bar Courtney ordered half a pint of Shipstone's for himself and a Bitter Lemon for Susan, and they stood for a few minutes drinking and attempting to continue the conversation they had been enjoying prior to entering the *Tavern*, but the noise was such that normal conversation was impossible, so they decided to take their drinks outside with them to enable them to talk. As they were on their way out, however, the girl who was with Susan's former boyfriend commented, 'Look at that bleddy cheap slag!' Susan swung round, but Courtney grabbed her by the arm, saying softly, 'Leave it – take no notice!' and escorting her out of the bar.

Hardly had they got outside, however, than the bar door swung open again and four young men emerged and brusquely confronted Susan's boyfriend. 'Look here, you black trash,' one of them said, pushing his face right into Courtney's. 'We've had enough of you lot coming over here and taking our jobs and pinching our girls – why don't you get off back to the jungle!'

'Yes, back up into the trees where you came from,' said another.

Courtney tried to keep calm and said nothing, but, feeling the other's nose pressing uncomfortably into his, raised his hand slowly with a view to pushing the intrusive head away. That move, however, was sufficient to prompt a swift and violent reaction: two of the aggressor's three companions swiftly produced flick knives from their pockets, while the fourth drained the pint glass he was holding, bashed it against the pub wall in order to transform it into a particularly vicious weapon, and then smashed the resultant jagged edges into Courtney's face. Courtney screamed as blood spurted from his face; Susan screamed even louder. Suddenly there was a stream of white youths who came running out of the pub and a crowd of black youths who had appeared seemingly from nowhere, and a pitched battle ensued, in which Courtney and Susan played no part, for Courtney was lying on the pavement with Susan kneeling beside him trying to staunch the bleeding from his face wound with a towel which the publican had brought out; he, meantime, had gone back into the pub to call first an ambulance and then the police.

The ambulance arrived long before the police, quickly followed by three or four more ambulances, for Courtney was by no means the only casualty. Susan accompanied Courtney into the ambulance and went with him to the City Hospital. By the time the police arrived there was a full-scale riot in progress; according to some accounts there were as many as a thousand involved, and eight men, in addition to Courtney, were taken to hospital – one needing as many as thirty-seven stitches to a wound in his throat, having been pushed into a window.

It was several hours before the police were able to restore order to the streets of St Ann's; as the *Nottingham Evening Post* reported the following day, 'it was like a slaughterhouse'. The national press, with one voice, called the occurrence the 'Nottingham race riots'; the Chief Constable of the city, Captain Althelstan Popkess, denied the following day that there had been any racial aspect to the disturbance however, although the residents of St Ann's knew better. The end of the economic boom meant that there was increasing competition for jobs, and a series of attacks on West Indians – including, according to the local press, an attack on a black man while he was out getting medicine for his pregnant wife – had put the black community on their guard, which explained the promptness with which they reacted.

Susan, of course, accompanied Courtney to the hospital and remained there until it had been confirmed that he would have to stay at least overnight, but that his life was not in danger; the lacerations to his face and neck, however, were so severe that he needed nineteen stitches. As she was not a relative, she was not allowed to be with him while he was treated, nor after he had been moved to the ward, but nevertheless she stayed at the hospital until two o'clock in the morning, when she was finally told to leave; the only further information she was able to elicit was that he was now sleeping.

The hospital, however, was at least three miles from home and, of course, at that time of night there were no buses, even on a Saturday night; nor was there any possibility of her taking a taxi – in fact the thought never even crossed her mind, for she simply had not enough money to pay the fare and in any case she had never travelled by taxi in her life. Walking was therefore the only option, so, having enquired of a hospital porter in which direction she should walk, she set off. By the time she arrived home, footsore, weary and still upset because of the evening's events, it was already half past three.

Susan was surprised to see that the house was not in darkness as she had expected. She let herself in, and seeing that the kitchen light was still on, she went in and was immediately confronted by her angry mother.

'What bleddy time do you call this then?' her mother shouted. 'And just look at you – you look as if you've been pulled through a hedge backwards! You've got blood on your face too – what's he done to you?'

'Who?'

'That black man you've been out with all night! Where've you been to until this time?'

'I've been at the hospital since about eleven o'clock…'

'Wilfred, I told you no good would come of her going out with men like that! What's he done to you, poor lamb? Come and let's have a look at your face.'

'He's not done nothing to me! Give over, will you! He's the one that was hurt, not me – if you can see blood on my face, it's his, not mine! And I'm proud of it too, and proud of him!'

'You shameless hussy! What did I tell you, Wilf? I told you she was asking for trouble going round with men like that, didn't I?'

Wilf said nothing; he had learned a long time ago that when Cissy was in this kind of mood she was not expecting answers to any of the questions that issued from her lips, and on balance it was better to say nothing. In any case Cissy appeared not to have noticed his lack of reply and she resumed her tirade regardless, feeling confident, in the lack of any evidence to the contrary, that she had her husband's backing. But as soon as she heard her mother's voice again, Susan started screaming with rage.

'Can't you just shut up for a minute while I tell you what happened? Why do you always decide that I'm in the wrong before you know anything about what happened? Are you my Mam or not? I'd have thought a mother would at least want to know why her daughter's had to spend half the night taking her boyfriend to hospital because she's afraid he's going to die! And I've had to leave him there overnight and walk home all on my own! All the way from the City Hospital too, not the General, though that would have been bad enough! Poor Courtney had to have nineteen stitches in his face because some filthy youth who was so drunk he could hardly stand up smashed a beer glass into his face...'

'Well, you can't say I didn't warn you – that's what these darkie lads are like...'

'He's not a darkie, he's black! And the boy that did it was white! Don't you ever listen to a word I say? No, you don't – it's no good talking to you! I'm going to bed!'

Susan rushed out of the room trembling with rage and with tears streaming down her face, slamming the door behind her as she went.

'You shouldn't be so hard on her, you know...' Wilf ventured.

'What do you know about it? What do you know about anything! You never say anything to back me up – no wonder she's out of control!'

At that Cissy too left the room, with yet another slam of the door. Wilf stayed where he was for a while; he hated unpleasantness, especially if it involved having a row with Cissy. As a result he tended to allow Cissy to say things and do things which he felt were unjustified or uncalled for, because experience had taught him that even if his point of view was incontrovertibly correct, she was sufficiently skilled in argument to prove herself right and him wrong. On this occasion he had actually been much more supportive of his wife than was his habit, although she was unlikely to have noticed; it was not so much that he disagreed with her concerns, but, left to his own devices, he would have been rather more diplomatic in expressing them.

His habit of following the line of least resistance was a fault he recognised in himself, but one which he was unable, or perhaps even unwilling, to eradicate, preferring a quiet life to the alternative of constant disputes in which he would always be found to be in the wrong. One consequence of his tendency to remain silent was that it implied that he agreed with Cissy and that he supported her actions, even on occasions when he did not; as a corollary she never even seemed to notice when he did express his support. She was not a bad woman, but Wilf thought in particular that she took too hard a line with their daughter, and although he had been far from outspoken tonight, it was rare for him to be as bold as he had been in expressing his feelings. He waited downstairs for twenty more minutes or so and it was only after having checked that all was quiet upstairs, and that the bedroom light had been switched off, that he went upstairs himself and slipped into bed alongside the now sleeping Cissy.

The following morning, it being Sunday, Wilf and Cissy had a lie-in. It was not something they normally did, but they had been up half the night waiting for and worrying about Susan, and, even though they went to sleep fairly soon after their heads first hit the pillow, the emotionally draining altercation which had followed Susan's return took its toll, and it was already noon when Wilf got up and prepared Cissy's 'early morning' tea. They assumed that their daughter was still asleep, for there was no sound or sign of any movement. At length, seeing that it was already half past one and Susan had still not appeared, Cissy decided to investigate.

She was about to open Susan's bedroom door, but, fearing the renewed hostility with which her intrusion might be greeted, she knocked first. There was no answer. She knocked again, louder this time, but still there was no reply. Only then did she open the door and discover that, although Susan's bed showed signs of having been slept in, it was now unoccupied and, moreover, no one was in the room but herself.

'Wilf!' she called, 'Come up here!'

Wilf did his wife's bidding and went upstairs, asking as he went, 'Why? What's wrong, Cissy?' for he could tell from her tone that Cissy was in a state of some agitation.

'Susan's not here!' she answered.

Wilf went into the bedroom and saw for himself. 'She must have gone out then, because she's not downstairs,' he said. That was little more than stating the obvious, because there were only two bedrooms, and no bathroom, so unless she was hiding in the airing cupboard she could not have been upstairs; her own room was too small for there to be any hiding-places, and if she had been downstairs Wilf would have seen her.

'Well, where the dickens is she?' asked Cissy.

'How should I know? Your guess is as good as mine,' Wilf answered. 'But if you ask me, given that she was late home last night because the lad she was with was in hospital, I would guess that that's where she's gone.'

'No, I don't reckon so. Hospitals don't have visiting in the morning – they wouldn't let her in. Why don't you go down to that pub she was in last night?'

'She won't be there if the lad's in hospital!'

'He might not still be in hospital. She only said she'd had to leave him there overnight. He might have come out this morning, and now I'd bet my bottom dollar they've gone to the pub again. Go and have a look – I'm really worried in case he starts a fight again!'

Wilf was less than convinced that if Courtney had been released from hospital that morning they would have both returned to the place where he had been set upon, but he reluctantly agreed to go and have a look. When he arrived there, he found that the pub was closed, because there had been a great deal of damage caused the previous evening, and they had not yet been able to restore the premises to a state where they could resume normal trading. He was able to speak to the publican, however, but the publican was unable to give him any useful information other than that he had not seen either of them since the previous evening.

For Wilf to have seen his daughter, however, he would have had to go out more than three hours earlier, for it had been ten o'clock when Susan had gone out; despite her lack of sleep she had awoken early and was unable to get back to sleep, so full was her mind with thoughts of the previous day's events and with concern for Courtney's welfare. Ultimately she had decided to go over to the hospital, even though she suspected that they would be unlikely to let her see him, but at least, she thought, she would be able to find out whether he was still there. Fortunately she did not need to repeat her long midnight walk, for the buses were running. There was not, of course, a direct bus connection between St Ann's and the City Hospital, but there were two trolleybus routes which ran past the *Chase Tavern*; their ultimate destination was Wilford Bridge, which was at the opposite side of town to the hospital, but at least they passed through the centre of the city, and after getting off the trolleybus there, she would be able to catch a petrol bus in the Market Square to take her the rest of the way.

On arriving at the hospital she presented herself at Reception and asked for news of Courtney but, as soon as they learnt that she was not related to him, they refused to give her any information at all. She tried to argue, but, just as it was becoming clear to her that it was a lost cause, a door opened and Courtney suddenly appeared, his head swathed in bandages; she rushed towards him and he wrapped his arms around her.

'I'm on the way home,' he said.

'Are you sure you're fit to go home?' she asked.

'Oh yes, I'm fine, and there's nothing else they can do for me here until the stitches are ready to come out, so I'd only be getting in the way if I stayed here.'

'How are you getting home?'

'By bus, I suppose. I hadn't really thought about it, because they only told me I could go about a quarter of an hour ago. I have no idea what bus I need. How did you get here?'

'By bus – so at least I'll be able to make sure you get home safely. There's a bus that will take us into town, and then we'll change onto a 40 or 47 trolleybus. Are you sure you're okay to walk to the bus stop?'

'Oh yes, there's nothing wrong with my legs – it's only my face which is a bit of a mess... I did have a headache as well when I woke up this morning, but they gave me some aspirin or something, and it's okay now.'

So they walked out of the hospital arm in arm and went to the bus stop, where they only had ten minutes to wait before a green and cream double-decker bus appeared; they got on, sat side by side on the lower deck and resumed their conversation. In no time at all, it seemed, it was time for them to get off the bus; in fact the journey had taken about twenty-five minutes, and Little John, the clock on the dome of the Council House in Nottingham's Old Market Square, was striking two o'clock. They transferred to a trolleybus which took them along St Ann's Well Road, and alighted just one stop beyond where Susan had got on the bus earlier that morning, then walked a little way before they came to the street in which Courtney lived.

'I don't know what my old man's going to say to me,' Courtney said. 'He would have been expecting me to come home last night, and I wasn't able to let him know I was in hospital. He'll be out of his mind! Do you mind coming in with me? I think it might be easier for me if you're there too!'

'Yes, I'll come in with you if you're sure he won't mind,' Susan replied. 'But I wouldn't like to make things worse. Surely he won't be mad with you when he knows what happened?'

'Ha! You can never tell.'

By that time they were at Courtney's front door. He turned the doorknob, opened the door, and invited her in.

Before Susan even set eyes on Courtney's father, she heard him shouting. 'Where do you think you've been? What time do you call this?' And then, before his son had time to make any answer, 'What have you done to your head?'

'I'm sorry, Pa, I couldn't let you know – I had to spend the night at the City Hospital. Somebody smashed a beer glass into my face...'

'I hope you weren't fighting, Courtney...'

'No, Pa, I wasn't. If I'd been fighting I'd have been better off, because I'd have seen it coming. The first thing I knew was when I felt a bang on my head and I felt blood running down my face. And Pa, this is Susan. She looked after me and took me to hospital.'

'Are you a nurse?'

'No, just a friend,' Susan replied.

'So who was the guy who hit you, and why did he do it?'

'I don't know who it was, and I don't know why he did it.'

'There must have been a reason. People don't just attack people for no reason…'

'Sometimes they do… Perhaps it was because I'm black…'

'And because you were with a white girl, is that it?'

'I don't know, Pa. Maybe it was…'

'Where did it happen?'

'We were at the *Chase Tavern*, at the corner of St Ann's Well Road and Robin Hood Chase.'

'I told you to keep away from pubs. That's asking for trouble! So how many people were fighting? Was it just you, or three or four of you?'

'No, a lot more than that! I didn't have time to count them, but there were a few hundred…'

'A few hundred? Don't tell me lies, man!'

'I'm not lying, Pa – there were crowds of people fighting, and as many black as there were white…'

'If there were as many people as that fighting, why didn't the police come?'

'They did. But there were too many people fighting – they couldn't do anything to stop it.'

Courtney went on to relate to his father exactly what had happened before the incident, how he had been attacked and then taken to hospital by ambulance, taking good care to ensure that he gave Susan full credit for staying with him for as long as the hospital staff would allow and then returning to the hospital the following morning. Mr Reid thanked her politely, but for the rest of the time she was there, he paid little attention to her presence, and she felt so uncomfortable that she made virtually no contribution to the conversation.

It was a few days before Susan and Courtney met again, for Courtney was not well enough to go out, and Courtney's father had made it clear that he was no more enthusiastic about the notion of mixed-race relationships than were Susan's parents. So, while Susan was on the receiving end of a barrage of criticism from her parents, especially her mother, Courtney was engaged in a similar battle, although Mr Reid's objection was motivated more by prudence than by prejudice. When they did go out together again, they were careful to avoid the *Chase Tavern,* and all the other pubs in St Ann's come to that, choosing to spend their time in slightly more anonymous venues in the city centre, even though they were more expensive.

On the night of Saturday 30th August, exactly one week after the *Chase Tavern* incident, there was more trouble in St Ann's, with 4,000 people fighting in the street this time, many of whom were arrested, but Courtney and Susan were not there to witness the riot; nor indeed were many of the black community, for they too stayed out of trouble, leaving the young whites to fight among themselves; despite that undisputed fact, the events continued to be called 'the Nottingham Race Riots' by the national press.

Racial tension remained very much in evidence in the Broadhurst household however, with Cissy in particular harassing her daughter at every conceivable opportunity. Wilf, however, held back, at least as far as Susan was concerned; he refrained from berating her when they were alone, although he never went so far as to condone her friendship with Courtney, being too worried that, in the course of one of the constant rows between mother and daughter, Susan might go so far as to boast that she at least had the support of her father, and so play one off against the other. When he was alone with his wife he was equally careful to avoid expressing specific support for Susan as far as her relationship with Courtney was concerned, restricting himself to suggesting to Cissy now and again that she ought to go easy on Susan, and warning her that she was running the risk of losing her altogether. Needless to say, Cissy did not welcome Wilf's comments, but as long as he restricted himself to speaking in general terms her reactions were less vehement than they might have been, and overall, he felt he could cope with that.

By the end of September the animosity between mother and daughter had become almost tangible and, early one Friday evening, after a whole hour devoted to a particularly vituperative slanging match, punctuated as usual by violent door-slamming, Susan stormed out of the house. She walked a little way up the road, then turned left into St Bartholomew's Road and followed it right to the end; there, at its junction with St Ann's Well Road, she found Courtney waiting for her, even though there was still fifteen minutes to go before their appointed meeting time.

'You're here early!' she said.

'So are you!' he replied. 'And you look hot and bothered – have you been crying?'

'I don't seem to do much else these days, except when I'm with you! I suppose my eye make-up's run, has it?'

'Yes, just a bit. What have you been crying about tonight?'

'Oh, the usual thing – I had a blazing row with my Mam and Dad.'

'That's nothing new.'

'I know, but it was worse than usual. Oh look, here comes a trolleybus – let's go as far as Wilford Bridge and then have a walk by the river.'

As soon as they boarded the bus Susan took a compact from her handbag and repaired her make-up, then turned her attention back to Courtney.

'Are things any better for you at home?'

'No, not at all. My Pa had a letter from my Mom in Jamaica this morning, and she's worried about me, he says, so he started having a go at me again.'

'What's your Mam worried about?'

'She thinks I'm still a little boy really. Well, I was the last time I saw her, so I suppose she doesn't know

I've changed. She thinks I'm too young to start going out with girls...'

'But you don't go out with girls – you go out with me...'

'I know. But the fact that I'm going out with just one girl seems to make it even worse than if I went out with a lot. She thinks I'm too young to settle down.'

'Does she know you're going out with a white girl?'

'Oh yes. That's something else she keeps going on about...'

'Doesn't she like white girls?'

'She doesn't know any. But she's worried about what will happen if I marry a white girl and we have children, because she says the children won't be black, but they won't be white either, so they'll grow up with nobody liking them.'

'But what do you think? That's the thing that matters to me!'

'I don't care what colour they are – if I have children I'll love them anyway!'

'And does your Dad think the same as your Mam?'

'About that, yes. But at least he doesn't treat me as if I'm still a little boy. But he worries about any children I have, because he's afraid they'll be unhappy.'

'And what about his own child? Are you happy?'

'I'm happy when I'm with you, but I'm not happy with all the rows that go on at home.'

'Well, I'm desperately unhappy, and the only time I'm happy is when I'm with you! What gets me is that our parents worry too much about our kids being unhappy, even though they haven't been born yet, but they couldn't care less whether we're happy ourselves! And then there's your Pa – he doesn't like me very much, does he?'

'I don't think you can say that. He's never said he doesn't anyway.'

'Well, the only time I've ever met him was when you came home from hospital, and he asked me if I was a nurse, and after that he completely ignored me...'

By this time their trolleybus had reached the terminus, so they got off and began strolling along the riverbank in the direction of Trent Bridge. For a few minutes they walked in silence, then Susan resumed the conversation they had been having while on the bus.

'I've had enough!' she declared. 'What say we run away together?'

'Run away together? We can't!'

'Why not?'

'Where would we go?'

'We could go to London... If we went to London they wouldn't be able to find us. London's a big place.'

'I know it is. But we don't know a soul in London...'

'I know. And that's a very good reason for going. We'd be able to choose our own friends and do our own thing.'

'But we've got no money! How would we live?'

'We could get a job…'

'Where?'

'Oh, I don't know… Anywhere! We've both got jobs already, haven't we?'

'Yes, but…'

'And if we can both find jobs in Nottingham why can't we both find jobs in London?'

'I don't know…'

'You don't seem very keen on being with me… I thought you said you loved me.'

'I do!'

'So why don't you want to be with me?'

'I didn't say I didn't want to be with you. It's just that I'm worried about taking a step in the dark…'

'It wouldn't be dark for long! Do you think we wouldn't be happy together?'

'No, of course I don't! But I don't like the thought of putting our own happiness before the happiness of our parents…'

'What do they care about us? All they do is nag all the time! Aren't you fed up with all the constant rows?'

'Yes, of course I am. I'm as fed up as you are.'

'So what's wrong? What's stopping you? Do you love your parents more than you love me?'

'No… Well, it's different…'

'Well, make up your mind – I'm going to run away anyway, whether you come with me or not!'

'Oh! Please don't go without me!'

'I don't want to… Especially now I know that I'm…' She hesitated before completing her sentence.

'Now you know what?'

'No, it wouldn't be fair, I'm not going to tell you…'

'What wouldn't be fair? What aren't you going to tell me? And why?'

The only answer Susan would give was to burst out crying and bury her head in her hands.

'Look, Susan, what's the matter? Please tell me! What have I done wrong?'

'You've not done anything wrong. I'm the one that's in the wrong – I shouldn't have mentioned it…'

'Mentioned what?'

'The fact that I'm pregnant…'

'Pregnant?'

'Yes. Don't you know what that means? I'm going to have a baby…'

'Yes, I know what it means, but how…'

'You know very well how!'

'And am I the father?'

'What sort of girl do you think I am? Of course you're the father! Or do you think I'm the sort of girl that sleeps around with any man that'll have her?'

'No, of course I don't think that! What are we going to do about it?'

'I'm not getting rid of it, if that's what you're thinking!'

'I wasn't thinking anything of the kind! So where do we go from here?'

'Well, my parents wouldn't have me in the house once they'd found out I was pregnant! What about yours?'

'Mine wouldn't either.'

'In that case there's only one thing to do…'

'What's that?'

'Do you want to live with the mother of your baby or not?'

'Of course I do!'

'So tell me how that's going to happen if we stay in Nottingham? No, there's no other way, we've got to go to London, and we've got to go as soon as we can, before it shows…'

'What do you mean?'

'Oh, don't you know anything? I mean before everybody can see I'm having a baby…'

'When will that be?'

'Oh, I don't know… Soon, anyway. I think we've got to go tomorrow morning…'

It was some time before Susan was able to convince Courtney that running away was the best option for them, but eventually she wore him down and, by the time they boarded the bus which would take them back to St Ann's for what Susan hoped would be the last time, they had a plan in place.

It was well after midnight when Susan returned home, by which time her parents were already in bed, Wilf having for once been able to persuade his wife not to pursue their quarrel throughout the night. When they got up the following morning, however, there was no sign of Susan and, when they eventually decided to enter her bedroom they found it was empty: the bed showed no sign of having been used, and Susan's wardrobe and chest of drawers had been cleared. On top of the chest of drawers was a brief, hastily scrawled note: 'I've had enough. I'm going to London with Courtney. Susan.'

Somewhat to Wilf's surprise, Cissy's reaction was to burst into tears. 'Perhaps you were right, Wilf. Perhaps I was too hard on her. I'm sorry,' she said, after which she burst into tears again.

Wilf did his best to console her, but to little effect, because he too was distraught; at least, however, he managed not to exacerbate the feelings of guilt which were overwhelming his wife. 'I'll go down to the station,' he said. 'I don't know what time the London trains go, but you never know, I might be able to find them and stop them doing anything silly.'

So Wilf went out, caught a trolleybus in St Ann's Well Road which took him all the way to the Midland Station in Carrington Street where, to his delight, he found that a train for London was due to depart in fifteen minutes' time and had not yet arrived. He bought a platform ticket and hastened down the steps to the platform, where he found about a hundred people were waiting for the London train. He walked up and down several times scrutinising each potential passenger, but there was no sign of Susan and Courtney. The train came, stayed at the platform just long enough for the passengers to board, but he still saw no sign of the runaway couple. The train drew out and Wilf made his way out of the station with a heavy heart.

Meanwhile, Courtney and Susan were sitting on a totally different train, which they had caught at a totally different station. Fearing that her father would indeed go to the Midland Station to try to waylay them, Susan had suggested that, instead of travelling to London St Pancras, which was the most obvious route, they should go to the Victoria Station and catch a train following the rather slower route, via Leicester and Rugby, to London Marylebone. They still needed to be very watchful in case Wilf had anticipated their plan, but when the train drew into the station there had been no sign of him, and the young couple breathed a sigh of relief and boarded the train; their new life together was about to start.

Initially it did not worry Susan too much that she had hoodwinked her boyfriend into going away with her; for she was not in fact pregnant. To her way of thinking, her lie was a legitimate stratagem to help him make up his mind; he had, after all, assured her that he loved her and wanted to be with her, and, once Susan had told him that she was carrying her baby, he seemed to have no regrets. During the journey, however, he appeared so solicitous, so intent on ensuring her comfort, that she began to feel guilty about deceiving him. At that stage, however, her principal worry concerned the way she might explain herself when, in a few months' time, no baby materialised; when that did eventually happen a couple of months later, she pretended to be as incredulous as Courtney, but, far from pleading guilty to deceiving him, she was able to get away with blaming it on an obviously incompetent doctor, who, she claimed, had told her that she was in the early stages of pregnancy. It was not until some considerable time later that she reproached herself for her callousness and for the way in which she had effectively treated his father, because whereas she had threatened to leave home on countless occasions, Courtney's departure had come like a bolt out of the blue for Mr Reid; even so, she never acknowledged her fault to a living soul.

Back at Bluebell Hill Road, Wilf and Cissy were at their wits' end; sometimes their distress manifested itself through periods of petty niggling, very occasionally through heated, clamorous quarrels, and, at times, through moments of tender understanding. Their discomfort was intensified by a feeling of utter helplessness; by a desperation which made them willing to go to any lengths to undo the damage which they recognised as having been caused by their own intransigence. This, however, was invariably followed by an immediate feeling of frustration that whatever they did would be to no avail, for if they did not know the whereabouts of Susan and Courtney, no reconciliation was even remotely possible.

This did not prevent Wilf from doing what he could. He went to the police to ask them to register

Susan as a missing person, but, even though they made a lot of notes and promised to do what they could, he left the police station with the distinct impression that their note-taking was just for show, and that they felt they had rather more important issues on which to utilise their resources. He went to see Eric Irons, a leading member of Nottingham's Jamaican community who was destined to become the country's first black magistrate, but, although Mr Irons treated him with the utmost courtesy and respect, he was also at a loss to make any useful suggestions concerning lines of enquiry.

Wilf even considered going to London to look for them, and went so far as to think about buying a copy of the *Geographers' A–Z Street Atlas* of London, but one glance inside was enough to convince him of the futility of his idea – if he had taken the trouble to count London's streets he would have discovered that they number more than 60,000. Even if the young couple had remained in Nottingham, he told himself, he would have no idea where to start searching for them, so what chance would there be in London? And, of course, although Susan had said in her farewell note that they were going to London, there was every possibility that it might not be true, for he knew her well enough to be aware that she was eminently capable of telling what she considered to be a 'white' lie if such a thing should be needed to fulfil her purpose; they might have gone to Leicester, or

Birmingham, or Manchester – in truth the list of possible destinations was almost infinite.

But what if, he asked himself, they had not even left St Ann's? In that case Susan would probably have turned up for work as usual. He knew nothing at all about Courtney, not even his surname, but it was improbable that a young Jamaican immigrant would be able to support two people, considering the level of pay normally offered to such workers, so Susan would be unable to give up her own job; she worked as a pay clerk in the Boot's head office in Station Street, near the Midland Station. He was, however, unable to go there to ask whether she had turned up for work or not, because he needed to be at work himself. He too worked at Boot's, of course, but the Island Street site where he worked was some way from Station Street; it did occur to him however that a Boot's employee at Island Street could easily call Head Office – if they were senior enough to have access to a telephone, which Wilf was not. Even so, he unburdened himself to his foreman, with whom he was on fairly good terms, for they had been at school together. The foreman promised to have a word with the under-manager, the under-manager called Head Office, spoke to the Senior Wages Clerk, and then went himself to relay the outcome of his call to Wilf.

It transpired that Susan had not been seen at work since the previous Friday. Since it was now Wednesday, she had therefore been absent from work for three days. Moreover, as the Senior Wages Clerk was speaking to a manager, he was willing to divulge one piece of information which he would in all probability not have revealed to Wilf: another pay clerk had also been absent over the same period, a young Jamaican named Courtney Reid.

Although the information conveyed to him by the under-manager did not advance his search significantly, Wilf felt a strange sensation of relief, for he had established beyond reasonable doubt that Susan and Courtney had gone away – if they had not left Nottingham, they would not have failed to turn up to work. What was more, he now knew Courtney's surname.

That evening, after returning home from work, he had tea and then went out. He had no specific plan, other than to go to a part of St Ann's where he knew there was a particularly large concentration of Jamaicans. He ventured down one street, where he saw there were a number of young boys playing cricket. He stopped and watched their game for a minute or two, then chose a convenient moment to approach one of them, the wicket-keeper, who seemed to be running the game. 'Do you know anybody called Reid?' he asked.

The boy eyed him with suspicion. 'Who wants to know?' he asked.

'My daughter has a friend who comes from Jamaica and who lives round here. His surname is Reid, and I need to find him. Can you help me?'

Observing that Wilf smiled as he asked, the boy felt sufficiently reassured to answer. 'Yes, my name's Reid.'

'Oh good,' replied Wilf, hardly able to believe his good fortune. 'Do you have a brother called Courtney?'

'No sir,' the boy answered respectfully.

'I do!' said one of the boys who had gathered around Wilf as soon as he had begun his conversation with the wicket-keeper.

'Oh, thank you!' Wilf cried, overjoyed. 'Is his surname Reid?'

'No, his surname is Clarke.'

Wilf's face fell and the entire group of boys howled with laughter. But Wilf persisted. 'Do you know anybody else called Reid?'

'Yes – me!' shouted one, followed by another, then another and another.

'Do any of you know anyone called Courtney Reid?'

They all shook their heads by way of reply, Wilf thanked them and left them to resume their game of cricket, having realised at last that Reid is one of the most commonly found surnames in Jamaica.

Eventually he returned home, having convinced himself that, sooner or later, Susan would just turn up on the doorstep, or at least get in touch, even if only to beg for financial help; in truth, after four or five days without her, they would have responded much more readily to such an appeal. Cissy felt sure that she would eventually return when she realised that her relationship with Courtney amounted to something less than a match made in heaven; Wilf, on the contrary, believed that Susan was sufficiently headstrong to persevere, even if not everything was perfect.

Meanwhile, Mr Reid, Courtney's father, was equally distraught, for precisely the same reasons, and he resolved to do what he could to contact Susan's parents. It was in fact a good deal easier for him to discover Wilf and Cissy's address, for Broadhurst was not a very common name, and, in addition, he already knew that they lived in Bluebell Hill Road; the fact that Bluebell Hill Road was a long road made very little difference, for Mr Reid's approach was systematic and logical. Assuming that the residents would know the surnames of at least their immediate neighbours, he knocked on the door of every fifth house, beginning at number 5, then progressing to numbers 10, 15, 20, 25 and so on; at each house he asked if they had any idea where Mr and Mrs Broadhurst lived. Every now and again there was no reply to his knock, although in some cases the slight twitch of a curtain betrayed unwillingness to answer rather than absence. No matter, he thought; he simply knocked on their neighbour's door.

At last his methodical approach showed signs of bearing fruit, for he learned from the occupants of number 50 that there were some people named Broadhurst who lived at 53. He immediately made his way to 53, but, however many times he knocked, he received no reply. Every day for two weeks, he returned and knocked again, but no one ever came to the door, so he resorted to writing a letter in which he stated who he was, apologised for troubling them, and asked them to contact him as soon as possible, because he was sure that they must be as worried about their daughter as he was about his son.

The letter arrived while Wilf was out; Cissy opened it, read it, burnt it – and never breathed a word about it to her husband. Neither did she tell him that, on a number of occasions, she had observed a black man approach the house, heard his knock at the door, and decided not to answer. Eventually both Mr Reid and Wilf stopped trying, each of them totally unaware of the lengths to which the other had been going.

What possible motivation could there be for Cissy Broadhurst to frustrate the efforts of these two distraught men? In truth she would have been puzzled if anyone had asked that question, for the effect of her actions on either of them never even entered her mind; she would undoubtedly have claimed that she would never deliberately hurt another human being, and would have been desperately upset herself if anyone were to suggest that she would. It was, in short, the unintended consequence of unthinking behaviour, the result of an instinctive reaction based on fear; like a good many white British people of her generation, she had never even met or spoken to a black person, and the very thought of speaking to one filled her with trepidation.

In other words, when she saw an unknown black man coming to knock on her door, it did not occur to her that it might be Courtney's father, and that his presence was occasioned by the very same emotions that were filling their own hearts and minds; because she did not even think who the unknown caller might be, it did not occur to her to tell Wilf about it either. If she had spoken to him about it, Wilf would undoubtedly have gone in search of Courtney's father and ultimately collaborated with him in his heart-rending quest to find his missing son and Wilf and Cissy's missing daughter. Such is the nature of prejudice: those who harbour it are not necessarily evil in their intentions, but sometimes its accidental consequences can be just as devastating as if the perpetrator really were motivated by malevolence.

But what of Mr Reid's letter? Clearly, once she had read the letter, she knew precisely who the caller was, and what was his purpose. So why did she continue to say nothing about the matter? Purely and simply because she felt ashamed at what she had done. In consequence, her sin remained with her for the rest of her life, gnawing away at her conscience in a way that ultimately caused her more suffering than she would have experienced if she had had the courage to make a full confession to her husband.

A Happy Christmas

When Susan and Courtney stepped off the train at London Marylebone, they had no idea what to do, or even where to go, even though they had spent a good portion of the journey time discussing the matter. Susan had never visited London in her life; in fact the only time she had ever travelled by train was when she had gone on a week's holiday to Mablethorpe, on the Lincolnshire coast, shortly after Wilf returned home from the war, and she had only the vaguest recollection of that, having only just turned eight at the time. Courtney had at least visited London, but his knowledge of the capital was at best limited, for he and his father had stayed for a week or so in Brixton in 1948, when Courtney was no more than twelve. They had disembarked from the *Empire Windrush* at Tilbury, travelled by train to Fenchurch Street station, and been transported from there to Brixton in a bus, he remembered that, but after a few days living in a redundant air raid shelter in Brixton they had moved to Nottingham. Such was the extent of his knowledge of London.

During the early stages of Susan and Courtney's journey from Nottingham, Courtney had been pinning his hopes on being able to locate a cousin of his father's who lived in Lewisham, but there were a number of problems with that plan: in the first place he did not know his father's cousin's address, and did not realise how large an area the borough of Lewisham covered. And then, as Susan pointed out, even if they had been able to locate him, there was every likelihood that the cousin would immediately contact Courtney's father and reveal their whereabouts.

Eventually they resolved to make their way to Brixton, not just because that was where Courtney had begun the British phase of his life, but because they knew that there were a lot of Jamaicans living there, and, Courtney assured Susan, Jamaicans were by nature both friendly and helpful. Sure enough, when they first arrived there they saw plenty of Caribbean faces in the street as they walked round, but what they did not realise was that the transition from one London district to another can be quite abrupt, and they suddenly found themselves in a street where a number of houses displayed notices in their window offering rooms to let, but with the addition of an extra line: 'No Animals, No Blacks, No Irish', so they quickly retraced their steps. Ultimately they came to a church outside which a crowd of West Indians were standing, for a wedding had been taking place; as the wedding party departed, Courtney noticed that the minister who appeared to have been officiating at the wedding service was himself black. He immediately went to see him and, in a matter of minutes, he and Susan had found themselves a temporary place to stay until they were able to find something a little more permanent.

Eventually they were able to find a bed-sit in a street just off Railton Road; they gave their names to their landlady as Mr and Mrs Reid, for the vast majority of people offering rented accommodation at that time would have refused to let to an unmarried couple. Not that Susan and Courtney did not want, or did not intend to marry; on the contrary, they would both have been willing to marry straight away, but for the fact that Susan had only just turned twenty, and it was not until 1969 that it became legal to marry under the age of twenty-one without parental consent. In one respect they were extremely fortunate: they were both able to find employment with the London County Council as wages clerks at County Hall, which was only a fifteen minute bus ride away. What was more, Susan had harboured a fear that their inability to provide references – because of the haste of their departure from Nottingham – would make it impossible to get a job. In the event, her fear turned out to be groundless, because their performance in a series of proficiency tests revealed their competence more convincingly than any reference could have done.

After six months or so, however, they found themselves obliged to leave their bed-sit, for they discovered that Susan was now genuinely pregnant. As a result they moved to a small rented flat in Lewisham, which meant that it took them twice as long to get to work, but at least there was still a direct bus service. Susan continued working until three months before her baby was due. By that time, she had already celebrated her twenty-first birthday, which meant that not only could she now get married without her parents' consent, but also that she would not have to bear the stigma, as it was still regarded in the 1950s, of being an unmarried mother. So Susan and Courtney married in early October at Lewisham Register Office, and on 3rd January 1960, Susan gave birth to a little girl.

From time to time both Susan and Courtney felt extremely sad that their parents were not sharing in the joy which they were each experiencing, but their sadness usually remained unspoken, and was never acted upon; in consequence neither Wilf and Cissy, nor Mr and Mrs Reid, were ever able to experience the delights of being a grandparent.

Chapter Three
Nottingham 1986

When Wilf retired from Boots at the age of 65, he and Cissy decided to move house, principally because they did not care much for the redevelopment of the St Ann's area. Up to that time their own house had not been affected, but, they felt, it was only a matter of time and, now that Wilf no longer needed to live near his place of work, it seemed to be a good time to move to a more congenial area. They could not afford to buy a house, of course, but they managed to find a place whose rent they could afford in Forest Fields, towards the eastern end of Berridge Road, just a little way from the old Apollo cinema.

Nineteen years had then elapsed since the fateful day when Susan had stormed out of the house, and in all that time they had had no word of what she had become. That did not prevent either of them from thinking about her, of course, and on the mantelpiece of their living-room they continued to have on display a now much faded photograph of Susan as an eight year old, sitting in the Mablethorpe sand hills and eating an ice cream cornet. Wilf and Cissy had long since ceased to fall out over Susan's departure, but it was at a not inconsiderable cost, for, although each of them spent several hours of each day wondering what had become of her, neither of them dared even to mention her name, for fear of rekindling the rancour which had been left smouldering in their hearts.

Their life together had never been exciting, and in Forest Fields they settled into a humdrum life, each establishing their own routine: in Cissy's case it was a matter of losing herself in the fictional world of television soap operas such as *Coronation Street* or *Emmerdale Farm*; for Wilf it was the footballing exploits of Nottingham Forest as, under the direction of Brian Clough, they were entering the most successful period of their history, culminating in two European Championships.

But in 1984 Cissy had suddenly started to lose weight and to feel permanently tired; for some time the doctors she consulted found it difficult to diagnose her problem. Eventually, just over a year after her symptoms appeared, they concluded that she was suffering from ovarian cancer; sadly the diagnosis came too late for any treatment to be effective, and she died in the Nottingham Womens' Hospital in July 1985.

Wilf missed Cissy enormously. Even though they rarely held real conversations, he missed the very silences, and he missed the sound of her beloved television soaps. After her death he made a point of switching them on every day. He never watched them, and would have been quite unable to recount any of the storylines; the most he could do was name one or two prominent characters, such as Ena Sharples, Albert Tatlock and Elsie Tanner, but he would have found it impossible to tell you whether they appeared in *Coronation Street, Emmerdale Farm,* or even *Dixon of Dock Green,* come to that – he could, however, have told you with some degree of confidence that none of them was a footballer. But what mattered more than anything else was keeping the overwhelming feeling of permanent isolation at bay, and he found, initially at least, that simply hearing the sound was sufficient to stop him feeling totally alone.

After a while, however, the sound of Cissy's favourite television programmes ceased to suffice, and once more the overwhelming sense of solitude started to envelop him to such an extent that he went to see his doctor for the first time since Cissy's death.

'So, Mr Broadhurst,' Dr Gleeson said, even before Wilf had uttered a word, 'how are you coping with life on your own?'

Wilf explained that, as far as everyday living was concerned, he was perfectly capable of looking after himself, cooking meals and doing the housework, for instance, even though he did not find it necessary to dust the furniture for more than an hour every morning, as had been Cissy's habit; he had after all got into the habit of doing everything, as soon as it was clear that Cissy was really ill, and he had actively enjoyed looking after her. But now, simply keeping himself busy was no longer enough; he simply felt lonely.

'Do you have many friends or relations?'

'Not really. All my relatives are dead – well, I do have a daughter somewhere, but I don't know where she is. We haven't seen her for the best part of thirty years...'

'Really? Why's that?'

'Oh, we had a big family row and she walked out on us – she said she was going to London, but London's a big place. We haven't even heard from her since.'

'How old was she when she left home?'

'Nearly twenty.'

'Oh, I'm sorry to hear that – you could do with her being around right now...'

'You're telling me I could! But, short of a miracle, that's not going to happen.'

'What about people you used to work with? Do you see any of them?'

'I sometimes bump into one or two of them if I go into town, but there's nobody I used to get on with really well that lives anywhere near me.'

'How often do you go out?

'Two or three times a week I go out to the shops, and every week I go to the Post Office to collect my pension.'

'Do you talk to anybody while you're out?'

'Not usually, apart from passing the time of day with shopkeepers and that.'

'Do you chat to anybody on the phone?'

'No, I don't have a phone. And I don't know anybody who has either.'

'Do you go to church?'

'No, I've never been one for going to church. I'm not really religious.'

'I don't think that really matters. The churches are full of people who aren't really religious – they just go for the companionship. I think it might do you good. I really think you need to get out more, and see more people. Do you have any pets?'

'No.'

'If you got yourself a little dog you'd have to go out every day. I think that would be a good idea, because taking a dog for walks is a very good way of meeting people.'

'I hadn't really thought about that.'

'Then you should.'

'Are you sleeping all right?'

'Yes, okay.'

'And there's nothing else worrying you?'

'No, not really.'

'Well, I don't think there's anything I can give you to make you feel better. Just take my advice and get out more. Church, dog – pub, for that matter. People need people – there's probably someone somewhere who even needs you!'

It was as a result of his visit to the doctor that Wilf bought a little dog, a little Jack Russell to which, in a sort of tribute to the factory where he had worked ever since his marriage to Cissy, he gave the name Boots. He was surprised to find how much he enjoyed having a pet to look after, and he talked to him endlessly. It didn't matter that Boots did not reply to what he said, for Wilf had long grown accustomed to Cissy's silences. In particular it gave Wilf the opportunity to talk about Susan, which he did regularly; in these conversations Boots's silence was a positive advantage, for it meant he could say whatever he liked about Susan – or about Cissy, for that matter – and not have to justify what he said or suddenly find himself forced onto the defensive.

One of the other advantages of having a dog was undoubtedly that it made him go out every day, whatever the weather. He made a point of changing the route of their walk regularly, which Boots did not appear to mind, although it was clear that the dog particularly enjoyed walks which took them onto the Forest recreation ground, the immense park-like area which was the location every October for the city's famous *Goose Fair*. Fortunately there were a number of different routes which they could follow to get to the Forest, and it was as a result of choosing an unfamiliar route that something happened that was to mark a turning-point in Wilf's life.

Wilf and Boots had gone down Birrell Road and turned right into Wiverton Road, with Wilf intending to cross the road straight away and turn right into Premier Road, which would lead them to the Forest, but for some reason Boots seemed reluctant to cross the road, and Wilf gave him his head, thinking that it would make no material difference if they turned left into Leslie Road instead, which was only fifty or so yards further on. As they were passing a newsagent's shop near the junction with Exeter Road, Boots was attracted by an interesting smell and insisted on stopping. Wilf allowed him to stop, and, while waiting for Boots's inquisitiveness to be satisfied, he began looking at a notice board outside the shop on which were displayed a number of postcards, most of which offered articles for sale.

Suddenly Wilf's attention was drawn to one which was headed:

I'M LOOKING FOR FATHER CHRISTMAS!

He read on and saw this appeal:

*'I'm looking for a kindly old gentleman who would dress up
as Santa Claus and visit children's Christmas parties.
Must be respectable and trustworthy, have a nice nature,
a smiley face and a sense of humour.
We will provide the costume.'*

The advertisement concluded with a telephone number and an address in Leslie Road.

By this time Boots was willing to move on; Wilf followed, and dog and master continued to make their way towards the Forest. As they went, Wilf thought about the advertisement he had just read. It was quite an appealing prospect, he thought, and not too arduous. He had not done anything of the kind before, however, and, he supposed, they would be expecting some sort of experience. Apart from that he seemed to fill most of the requirements: kindly – well, yes, he thought he was kindly, and he had a nice nature; old – yes, no doubt about that, nor about being trustworthy either. The only part of the description which made him hesitate was 'gentleman'. He would certainly not describe himself as a gentleman; that was for other people to determine, he felt.

He had not bothered to make a note of the telephone number, not because he was not interested, but because, as he had told Dr Gleeson, he did not have a telephone – had never had a telephone. As he had virtually no friends or relatives, and none of those he had possessed a telephone either, there was no point. If he really needed to call someone, there was no shortage at that time of public telephone kiosks. But he did have a good memory for addresses, and he remembered that the address mentioned was 15 Leslie Road. Just at that moment Boots decided to stop once more and, as Wilf was waiting, he glanced at the house in front of which Boots had stopped: it was number 15, and, what's more, they were in Leslie Road.

Wilf just stood there for a moment and reflected on what had just happened. Boots had made him change his mind about the route of their walk, otherwise he would not have seen the advertisement; then Boots had insisted on stopping alongside the shop's notice-board; and now he had obliged him to stop once more, right outside the house of the person who had placed the advertisement. No, he thought, don't be silly! A dog couldn't do that on purpose! And yet, and yet…

He opened the gate and began walking up the path which led across the tiny garden to the front door. Boots followed him, happily wagging his tail. Wilf rang the doorbell.

Wilf heard the click-clack of a woman's high heels and, a moment later, the door opened and he saw a young woman, wearing a smart summer frock – she was actually about thirty, but Wilf had reached that stage in life when everyone under pensionable age appears young. She looked at Wilf and said, 'Hello, what can I do for you?' Then, before Wilf could answer, she noticed the dog, said, 'Oh, what an adorable little dog!' and immediately bent down to make a fuss of him. 'What's his name?' she added.

'I call him Boots,' said Wilf, feeling suddenly embarrassed at having given his dog such a silly name.

'What a gorgeous name for a dog!' she exclaimed.

Wilf smiled, reassured. 'I used to work for Boots before I retired,' he explained, 'and I thought when I got him that Boots had been such a big part of my life that I would call him Boots too.'

'What a lovely story! And it suits him… Anyway, I'm sorry, what can I do for you?'

'It's just that I saw your advert for somebody to play Father Christmas,' Wilf began.

'Oh, I see. Well look, I'm just about to go out because my little girl comes out of school at a quarter to four and I need to be there to meet her. Is there any chance you could pop round to see me tomorrow morning?'

'Yes, that would be fine,' Wilf replied. 'What time?'

'Shall we say about ten o'clock?'

'Ten o'clock, yes, all right.'

'And bring Boots with you if you like…'

Wilf grinned widely and agreed.

'Just a moment,' the lady said. 'My name's Sheila Hardcastle – what's yours?'

'My name's Wilf, Wilf Broadhurst.'

'Okay, Wilf. Just let me give you one of these…' She disappeared for a moment, then returned and handed Wilf a leaflet. 'This will tell you something about the service we offer. There's one thing it doesn't say though, because this is really an information leaflet for clients who want to use our services – the normal fee for a Father Christmas visit is £15, but it depends how long the event lasts.'

Wilf's face fell. 'Do you mean I have to pay a fee?' he asked anxiously.

Sheila laughed. 'Good gracious, no! That's what we pay you!'

'Oh!' said Wilf. 'I didn't realise I'd get paid! Fifteen quid too!'

'Well, it is a job,' Sheila countered, 'and not many people would take a job without getting paid! Anyway, I must go – I'll see you at ten o'clock tomorrow, Wilf.'

She shook Wilf by the hand, then bent down once more to stroke Boots. 'Bye, Boots,' she said, 'see you tomorrow!'

'Goodbye,' said Wilf, 'see you in the morning.'

Sheila closed the door and Wilf and Boots began walking home, Wilf walking with an unaccustomed spring in his step. It was only when they arrived home that he suddenly realised that Boots had not completed his walk, so he turned round and took the little dog for a run around the fields of the Forest. Boots raised no objection.

When he returned home, Wilf had a look at the leaflet Sheila Hardcastle had given him, and was amazed at what he read, for the impression he received was that she had successfully established a professional business, providing entertainers of all kinds for children's parties: conjurors, musicians, clowns, comedians – and, of course, Father Christmases... in other words it was an all the year round business. Parents would organise a party for their child or children, either in their own home or in hired premises, and, in return for a fee, entertainment would be provided at the time and at the place they specified. It was a brilliant idea, thought Wilf, who had never even imagined that such a thing was possible; but, of course, times had changed, and with them desires, aspirations and opportunities. And now he might have a new opportunity himself, to dress up as Santa Claus and visit people's houses and bring

67

happiness to children; he beamed inwardly at the very thought.

The following morning Wilf and Boots left home at 9.30; they were not due at Sheila's house until 10 o'clock, and it was little more than ten minutes' walk, but Wilf knew Boots well enough to realise that he needed his own time. In point of fact, they arrived fifteen minutes early, for Boots did not stop once on the way, but wagged his tail enthusiastically as soon as they arrived at 15 Leslie Road.

'No, come on, Boots, we're too early,' said Wilf. 'We'd better walk round a bit.'

So they continued to the end of Leslie Road, turned left along Gregory Boulevard and walked as far as Foxhall Road before turning round and retracing their steps, arriving at Sheila's house on the dot of 10 o'clock.

'You're very punctual,' said Sheila when she opened the door. 'That's a good sign. Come in, Wilf – you too, Boots!'

Wilf and Boots followed Sheila into the hall, then turned left into the front room, a comfortable room with a bay window, a sofa, two armchairs and a piano. 'Sit down over there, Wilf. I just have a few questions I need to ask you before we go any further…'

'Okay,' replied Wilf, 'go ahead.'

There followed a fifteen minute interview during which Sheila asked Wilf a lot of questions about himself, where he lived, where he had worked and so on, before asking, 'Do you have much experience of children, Wilf? I expect you've got grandchildren, haven't you?'

'No, I haven't. Well, no… I don't know really… Perhaps I have, but I don't know them.' Almost before he knew it, he was relating the story of Susan having left home as the result of a dispute – he chose not to go into details concerning the reasons for the dispute – and how they had completely lost contact. 'Seeing as how she went to London with a boyfriend, I suppose she probably did have children of her own, but she never got in touch to tell us.'

'How do you feel about that?'

'Well, for a long time it was very hard, but there was nothing we could do about it, so we just got on with our lives. But I still sometimes sit and think of Susan and her family – I sometimes dream about them too…'

'How many grandchildren do you have in your dreams?'

'Oh, it's always different. Sometimes there's just one, sometimes there's half a dozen – but however many there are, there's always a little girl. And even if they only have one child, it's always a girl. I suppose that must be because Susan's a girl, and I've always missed her so much… Of course, Susan's children would all be grown up by now, I suppose, but I never dream of them as being grown up, they're always little in my dreams.'

'How old would Susan be now then?'

'Let's see... She was born in 1938, so she'd be 48 now, I suppose. Gosh! I'd never thought about that – I always think of her as she was the last time I saw her!'

'I can understand that. My goodness, you've had a bit of a hard time of it really, haven't you? And yet you seem a pretty cheery soul in spite of everything!'

'Well, you don't get anywhere if you sit in a corner moping, do you? That's not the way I am...'

'Good for you, Wilf. Now, about this job... If you're going to be one of our Father Christmases, it's not going to be all the year round, you realise that, don't you?'

'I hadn't even thought about that, but no, I can see that people wouldn't want Father Christmas to come in June or July, would they?'

'No, that's right. We get the occasional request in November, but of course mostly it's in December, with the odd one in early January.'

'Did you say one of our Father Christmases?'

'Yes, that's right.'

'How many do you have then?'

'We have three on our books at the moment, but last December we didn't have enough – we got asked to provide six on the same day, so we had to juggle the times around, and they each did two parties that day, which was pretty tiring for them. Now, I've got just one spare Santa suit at the moment, so I shall need you to try it for size. Do you mind going upstairs and trying it on?'

'Are you going to take me on then? Have I got the job?'

'I can't see any reason why not, can you?'

'No, not at all. Good Lord! Me as Father Christmas! What would Cissy say?'

So Sheila handed him the costume and showed him upstairs to a bedroom, where he put on the entire outfit, beard and all, before coming downstairs again ready for inspection.

'Wow!' said Sheila. 'That looks good – or it will with a little bit of padding, because Santa is supposed to be a bit on the chubby side! How does it feel?'

'All right,' said Wilf, 'except that bits of this beard keep getting in my mouth.'

'You'll soon get used to that,' Sheila assured him. 'In any case we can always snip the offending bits off to make it less uncomfortable. What do you think, Boots?'

But Boots made no reply; he was hiding behind the sofa.

'Come on, Boots,' said Wilf. 'It's only me!'

Hearing his master's voice Boots emerged from behind the sofa, and Wilf kept talking and stroking him until he eventually got used to Wilf's reincarnation as Santa Claus.

'Now, then,' Sheila said, 'it's going to be quite a while before you get called upon, unless someone decides to be a bit silly and have a Christmas party at the height of the summer – you never know! Normally I would give you a ring as soon as I get a booking, but

71

obviously I can't do that with you because you don't have a phone. But fortunately you don't live far away, so I'll just pop round to see you instead. Would that be all right?'

'Yes, of course it would be,' said Wilf. 'And I'm sure Boots would be happy if you did, because he seems to have taken quite a shine to you!'

'And me to him! Anyway, if you happen to be out when I come, I'll just pop the details through your letter box. But one piece of advice – if I were you, I'd try the costume on now and again, and keep it on for an hour or two, because it will take some getting used to! And you don't want to feel uncomfortable while you're doing a party, it's pretty important to be relaxed and just feel natural.'

'I see,' Wilf replied. 'But there's something I want to ask you about getting to these parties…'

'Yes?'

'Well, I haven't got a car or anything, so do I have to go on the bus dressed as Father Christmas?'

Sheila roared with laughter. 'Oh no,' she said, when she'd finally composed herself. 'What normally happens is that you get there fairly early and change into the costume when you get there. The hostess will usually show you to a bedroom, where you can change and wait until they're ready for you to make your appearance. And if the party is in a church hall or somewhere like that, there's bound to be an office or a cloakroom where you can put your costume on.'

'And what do I have to do while I'm there?'

'The hostess will…'

'Hostess?'

'Yes, the hostess is the lady who's running the party – usually the mother of the little girl or little boy whose party it is – and she will tell you what she wants. I've got a little leaflet here that I'll give to you with a number of suggestions, sort of dos and don'ts…'

'I see…'

'Are you worried about anything, Wilf?'

'Not worried, no, just a bit nervous really, that's all.'

'You're bound to be at first. It's a bit like going on the stage. But you'll soon get used to it, don't worry! As soon as you see the look on the children's faces, you'll relax and have as much fun as they're having, you'll see! Is there anything else?'

'No, I don't think so…'

'Well, if you think of anything, just drop by and ask. Otherwise I'll be in touch when we start getting bookings, which will probably be September or October time – the mothers usually start planning fairly early.'

At home that evening Wilf changed once more into the Santa Claus costume, including the padding which Sheila had provided him with, and – to the puzzlement of Boots – he spent the entire evening dressed as Father Christmas, only taking the costume off when it was bedtime. After that he got into the habit of dressing up twice a week, until, as Sheila had predicted, he began to feel completely comfortable.

One day towards the end of September, Wilf had just finished having breakfast and was about to take Boots out for a walk when he heard a knock at the front door. He answered the door and found it was Sheila.

'Hello, Sheila,' he said. 'Come in.'

Sheila followed Wilf into the living room where he offered her a cup of tea. 'No thanks,' she said, 'I've got a busy morning, I can't stop. I just wanted to let you know that I've got some bookings for you.'

'Bookings? So you mean more than one?'

'Yes – in fact we've got four!'

'Four! I suppose, as you've got four Father Christmases now, including me, that means we've got one booking each, does it?'

'Oh no, I mean I've got four bookings for you!'

'Four for me? That's unbelievable!'

'Yes, isn't that good! The first one's going to be on Saturday December the sixth, which is a bit early for Christmas, and it's a birthday party for a little boy...'

'Whereabouts is it?'

'It's in West Bridgford – I can't remember the address off hand. Can you manage that?'

'Oh yes, of course I can – I'll just go into town on the bus and then change onto a Bridgford bus...'

'Okay. Then there are two the next weekend, one on Saturday, the other on Sunday, and the fourth one will be on Sunday the fourteenth.'

'Let me get a piece of paper and I'll write those down...'

'No, you don't need to, I've got all the details here.' Sheila opened her handbag and took out an envelope which she handed to Wilf. 'Have a look at the details and make sure the timings are all right...'

'Oh, the timings will be all right, I don't get out all that much,' Wilf replied.

'Yes, but have a look anyway.'

Wilf obediently opened the envelope and scanned the four sheets of paper which it had contained – one sheet for each party. The second would be in a church hall in Hyson Green, which would be easy for him to get to; the third was to be in Mapperley, which would be a little bit more awkward to get to, and the final one was at a private house in Sherwood, which again was straightforward.

'Are those okay for you, Wilf?'

'Yes, they're okay – the Mapperley one's a bit awkward to get to from here, but I'll manage...'

'Well, if it's difficult for you, I should be able to give you a lift. The little girl's mother is a friend of mine, so it won't matter if I turn up too.'

'Oh, that's all right then. I've been practising wearing the costume quite a bit, and I'm getting used to it now, but I still feel nervous about doing it...'

'Oh, you'll be fine after the first one, you mark my words! Now I'd better make tracks – I'm supposed to be meeting a friend in town in ten minutes' time!'

After that Wilf did not hear from Sheila for quite some time. His daily life remained as humdrum as ever: housework, cooking – in a fairly unadventurous way – and taking Boots for walks. To this, however, he added dressing up as Father Christmas – not just in order to get used to wearing the costume, as Sheila had suggested, but in order to get into the character. Every evening, instead of switching on *Coronation Street*, or whichever programme Cissy would have been watching on that particular evening, he would don his costume and rehearse his appearance through the door, then pretend to be talking to children of his own invention, giving them names and characteristics, and finally giving them their presents. As time went on, his routine became gradually more elaborate – and more polished. On the first few occasions Boots would sit watching him, bemused; after two or three weeks, however, he usually did nothing more than open one eye, check that nothing untoward was happening, and then close his eye again and go back to sleep, until Wilf aroused him once more to take him for his late night outing.

One day in October, Wilf received a letter – a rare occurrence, apart from the occasional official communication to do with his pension or something of the sort, for there was no one he knew who would be likely to write to him. What is more, he was surprised to see that the envelope was addressed to Mr and Mrs Broadhurst, implying that the sender, whoever it was, did not realise that he was a widower. A thought flashed across his mind: could it be a letter from Susan, perhaps? The handwriting was not like hers, as far as he could remember, but so many years had elapsed since he had last seen her, that her style of writing might easily have changed beyond recognition. He opened the envelope and read the letter it contained, which was very short. It said:

Dear Mr and Mrs Broadhurst,

I am sorry to trouble you and for possibly wasting your time, but I am trying to contact the parents of a girl my son Courtney ran away with twenty-eight years ago. Her name was Susan Broadhurst, and I spent a long time trying to find them after they left Nottingham, but I was not successful.

I am writing to every person in Nottingham called Broadhurst that I can find in the electoral register, so most of the people I am writing to will not know what I am talking about. If you are one of those people, please forgive me for troubling you.

But if you are the right people, I beg you, please let me know.

Thank you,

Yours sincerely,

Ernest Reid

When he had finished reading the letter, Wilf's eyes were full of tears. He remembered the hours he had spent trying to locate Courtney's father, and the thought that Mr Reid was trying to find him at the same time was almost more than he could bear. He sat down immediately and wrote a reply:

Dear Mr Reid,

Thank you for your letter. You didn't waste my time, because I am the person you are looking for. I'm sorry to tell you that my wife died last year.

I too spent a lot of time trying to find you, but, although I found many West Indians called Reid in St Ann's, I didn't manage to find the right one.

I would like to meet you if you would like to meet me. Just let me know when and where.

Yours sincerely,
Wilf Broadhurst

He went out immediately and put his letter in the post. Two days later he received a reply:

Dear Mr Broadhurst,

Thank you for your letter. I am so relieved to find you at last. I have not heard from Courtney since he left. Have you heard from Susan?

I live in Hyson Green now, so I am not very far away from you. If you would like to meet me, I will be in the public bar of the Carlton, at the corner of Berridge Road and Noel Street, from 6 pm until 7 pm tomorrow, and every evening for seven days.

Thank you,
Ernest Reid

The Carlton, a pub which Mr Reid had chosen for their rendez-vous, was less than half a mile from Wilf's house, and that same evening, he summoned Boots, put on his lead, and they walked together in the direction of the Carlton. When they arrived, Wilf was astounded at the number of people there: it happened to be the opening day of the Nottingham Goose Fair, and the Carlton was one of the nearest pubs to the Forest, which is where men had been working since the beginning of the week to install all the roundabouts and sideshows, for the Goose Fair is one of the biggest fairs in the country. Nevertheless he made his way into the Public Bar, and immediately spotted a man with very black skin but with snow white hair, standing alone in a corner. He approached him rather nervously.

'Are you Mr Reid by any chance?'

There was another flash of white, emanating this time from the man's teeth, as he grinned to show his delight. 'Yes, I am,' he replied. 'You must be Mr Broadhurst.'

'Yes, I am,' said Wilf, holding out his hand. 'Can I get you a drink?'

'I've already got one, thanks. Let me get you one…'

'No – your glass is nearly empty anyway. I'll get you another one – what is it?'

'It's a light ale.'

'Okay, I'll have the same. Do you mind holding the dog for me?'

Mr Reid smiled again. 'Of course I don't mind – I love dogs. What's his name?'

'His name's Boots.'

When Wilf returned with the drinks, his companion was crouching down talking to the dog. 'Here you are, Mr Reid,' he said, holding out his glass.

'It's Ernest, if you don't mind – or even Ernie. That's what my friends call me, and I hope we can be friends…'

'Yes, me too. My name's Wilf. So have you heard anything from Courtney and Susan?'

'Not a word in twenty-eight years. Have you?'

'No. Same here. Not a dicky bird since the day she walked out.'

Then Wilf told Ernie more about the efforts he had made to find him, after which Ernie described the rather more systematic process he had gone through himself, including the fact that he had written a letter to Wilf and Cissy asking if they could meet.

'Oh,' said Wilf in surprise. 'I never saw a letter – are you sure you put the right address on it?'

'I think so. Some neighbours told me you lived at 53 Bluebell Hill Road.'

'Yes, that was the address all right, but we never got it – it must have got lost in the post.'

'I didn't put it in the post. I put it through the letter box myself.'

The truth was beginning to dawn on Wilf, and he began to feel uncomfortable. 'Well, I never saw it, Ernie, and if you put it through the letter box yourself I can only assume that my wife picked it up and never told me about it.'

'Would she have done that?'

'Yes, I'm afraid she might. If she did, I'm sorry...'

'But why would she have done that?'

'It can only have been because she didn't like the idea of our Susan going out with a black man – she was far more upset about it than I was. Let me try and explain. Cissy wasn't a bad woman. She just hadn't had anything to do with black people before, and they worried her – not because she had any reason to worry, just because she didn't know what they were like. It was different for me, because I'd met a lot of black fellas in the army during the war, and I'd worked with some at Boots too. She didn't understand, that's all – I'm sorry.'

'I understand, don't worry. It was a long time ago, and things have changed quite a lot. A lot of black folk felt the same about white people too.'

'What did you think about Courtney going out with a white girl?'

'I wasn't happy. Not because I'd got anything against white girls, or about white folk in general, but because I was afraid it would land him in trouble.'

'You were right – it did.'

'Yes, I know. And it was because I saw how Susan looked after him when he got hurt that I realised that she was a really nice girl. Did you meet Courtney at all?'

'No, I'm afraid I didn't '

'He was a decent guy too, very gentle. I can sort of imagine why they might have felt they had to run away, but I've never been able to understand why they never got in touch again.'

'No, neither can I.'

'I assume they got married, so they probably have children too.'

'Yes, I've often had that thought as well, in fact I often have dreams about it. I'd love to have grandchildren. I always thought that one day, once everything had calmed down, Susan would write to us, but she never did. I can understand her being angry at the time, because of all the rows and everything, and I can understand it lasting for a few weeks or even years afterwards, but it really hurts me when I think she might still be feeling angry after all these years.'

'Me too. Can I get you another drink, Wilf?'

'No thanks, I'd better get going and let Boots finish his walk. It's been really nice to meet you, Ernie. Thanks for getting in touch.'

'Nice to meet you too, Wilf. Would you like to meet again?'

'If you'd like to…'

'Shall we say same time, same place next week?'

'Okay, suits me – see you then…'

At their next meeting the following week, Wilf learned that Ernie too was now a widower, his wife having died from a heart attack about five years before. She had remained in Jamaica while Courtney's two younger brothers and two younger sisters were still at school, and had come to join her husband two years after Courtney had left home; their other children, who were now all married, had never felt inclined to come over to Britain, although Ernie and his wife had been back to Jamaica in order to attend all their weddings – Ernie thought it important to do so in order to compensate in some way for having been deprived of seeing his eldest son get married.

After that Wilf and Ernie met every week for a drink and a chat, and soon became good friends, although for some reason Wilf felt too embarrassed to tell him about what had become his alternative persona: Father Christmas. They did, however, frequently chat about Courtney and Susan and how they might have turned out, what their children might look like, where they lived, although most of what they said about them was, of course, mere conjecture, but each of them was aware of the deep sorrow which lay in the other's heart.

But one day Ernie asked Wilf what his plans were for Christmas. Wilf replied that he had no plans, because he had no one to go to, and no one to invite.

'So what did you do last year?' asked Ernie.

'Nothing really. It was too soon after Cissy passed away for me to start thinking about enjoying myself, so Christmas Day was just like any other day of the year really.'

'But it doesn't have to be like that this year, does it?'

'No, I suppose it doesn't – I hadn't even thought about it. What did you do last Christmas?'

'Nothing. It was a bit like it was for you, I suppose. What say we get together for Christmas Day this year?'

'Yes, why not? Your place or mine?'

'What's your cooking like?'

'Okay… but nothing special.'

'Well, what about coming over to me then, and I'll cook us a nice traditional Jamaican Christmas dinner?'

'What would that be – turkey?'

'It might be, or sometimes you might have roast lamb or roast beef, but most people would have curried chicken or curried goat. In my family, though, we've always had roast ham, served with rice and gungo peas.'

'What peas?'

'Gungo. We sometimes call them pigeon peas, and they're mixed with the rice, and they're quite spicy. Do you like spicy food?'

'It depends how spicy it is! I don't like food that makes you feel as if your mouth is on fire.'

'Don't worry, I won't make it like that, I'll make it quite mild, but still tasty.'

'Do you have Christmas pudding too?'

'Oh yes, it's pretty much the same as yours, but with lots and lots of fruit, and there's loads of booze in it too!'

'Sounds pretty good to me! Okay, I'll come!'

As Wilf walked home afterwards, he felt genuinely happy that he and Ernie had come to this agreement, especially because he had found the previous

Christmas extremely difficult to cope with; apart from the few days immediately following Cissy's death, it was without doubt the period when his spirits were at their lowest ebb. At last, he reflected, he had now removed the main obstacle presented by his new job: if he were really to succeed in his Father Christmas role by making a lot of little children happy, he needed some reason to be happy himself, for heaviness of heart would undoubtedly cancel out any desire to be jovial, and children were unlikely to be fooled by false joviality.

At last December arrived, and with it the events for which Wilf had been rehearsing for months. His first engagement would be on Saturday the sixth, and the party was to be held in a house in Fox Road, West Bridgford. So seriously did he take the job he had accepted that, on the Monday before, not only had he bought a street guide to Nottingham to ensure that he would not get lost on the way to the party, but he had rehearsed the journey the same afternoon; he was terrified that he might arrive late – or, even worse, that he might fail to turn up at all. In fact he found that getting to the party venue would be a good deal easier than he had envisaged: he caught a bus to the City centre, then changed onto a trolleybus bound for Trent Bridge. There he would get off, walk across the bridge which spanned the Trent, and Fox Road was just on the other side of the famous cricket ground.

The following day Sheila came to visit him to check that he knew exactly where and when he needed to go, and she was extremely impressed by the professionalism with which he had prepared himself for the event although, in truth, it was largely driven by a terror of doing something wrong. He was due to arrive at 5.30 pm, while the children were fully occupied having tea, and the hostess would show him to a bedroom where he would be able to change. In fact he stepped off the trolleybus at Trent Bridge at 5 o'clock exactly, which meant that he needed to convert a ten-minute walk into one lasting fully thirty minutes. This he managed to accomplish by spending two or three minutes looking in every single shop-window in Radcliffe Road, even those which contained virtually nothing – which accounted for most of them. If anyone had asked him afterwards what he had observed in the shop windows he would have been unable to reply, for he had not really been looking, his mind being focussed on nothing more than wasting twenty minutes.

He arrived at the house at exactly 5.30 and was about to ring the doorbell when the door opened, and a lady who introduced herself as 'Mrs Schofield, David's Mum' led him upstairs to a bedroom where he would be able to change. 'Make sure you're ready at six o'clock', she said, 'and when you hear the doorbell ring twice, come downstairs, and I'll show you into the room where the children are.'

'How many children are there?' he asked.

'Fourteen,' she replied, 'and I've put all their presents on the bed – they're all the same, so it doesn't matter who gets what!'

With that she disappeared, and Wilf began his now familiar routine of donning his costume, after which he counted the presents to check that there really were fourteen, then put them in his sack. By the time he was ready it was already five to six, so he sat on the bed waiting for the doorbell to ring, as Mrs Schofield had instructed. As he sat on the bed waiting, he could feel his heart pounding and his mouth had become quite dry. 'Don't be a chump,' he scolded himself. 'Control your nerves – they're only kids, they won't hurt you!'

Suddenly he heard the doorbell – once, twice. He got up from the bed, picked up his sack of presents, and made his way downstairs, where he saw Mrs Schofield waiting by a closed door. 'Okay?' she whispered.

'Okay,' Santa Claus replied.

Mrs Schofield threw open the door and cried in a loud voice, 'Children, look who's come to see you!'

A great cheer went up as the children rose from the chairs on which they had been sitting to have tea – such a din, in fact, that Wilf was convinced that there must be far more than fourteen present, and what on earth would he do if he ran out of presents?'

'A happy Christmas, children!' he bellowed, in a specially cultivated gruff but kindly voice. 'Which one's David?'

A little boy stood up and presented himself shyly; he was a pale, spindly five-year-old – and probably the quietest boy at the party. Father Christmas held out his hands and beckoned to him, laughing. 'What a pleasure it is to meet you, David!' he said. 'You've always been asleep when I've been here before, and I expect you'll be asleep when I come again on Christmas Eve! What would you like me to bring you then?'

'A train set,' David mumbled.

'Speak up, David! Father Christmas won't be able to hear you!' cried Mrs Schofield.

'A train set!' David yelled.

'David! Don't forget your manners!' his mother exhorted.

'A train set, please,' came David's answer – much reduced in volume this time.

'A train set!' Father Christmas repeated. 'I'll see what I can do – everybody seems to want train sets this year! In the meantime, I've got a little present for you to be going on with – it's not a train set this time, you'll have to wait till Christmas Eve for that!' He took a present from his sack, handed it to the little boy and patted him on the head, whereupon David retired to his seat with an obvious sense of relief that he was no longer the centre of attention.

Fourteen times Father Christmas dipped into his sack and pulled out a present, and each time he had a little chat with the boy or girl concerned, until all the presents were gone and it was Wilf's turn to experience relief, as he looked around and saw that every child was in the process of opening their parcel.

'Now!' Father Christmas announced. 'I must go and feed my reindeer, or they won't be able to fly me back to the North Pole.'

'Where are they?' asked one little girl.

'Oh, they're on the roof of course,' Santa replied. 'And I expect they're pretty hungry too. Does anybody know what reindeer eat?'

Immediately there was a hubbub as every child present shouted out a suggestion: corn, bread, milk, sausages – every foodstuff possible seemed to be suggested. At length Father Christmas held up his hand. 'No,' he said, 'I'm afraid you're all wrong! Shall I tell you what they really eat?'

'Yes!' they yelled as one.

'They eat songs,' he went on, 'songs that are sung by children. Does anybody know *Jingle Bells*?'

'Yes!' they shouted.

'All right, let's hear you sing it!

And so they sang: 'Jingle, bells, jingle, bells, jingle all the way…'

'That was pretty good,' said Father Christmas after they had reached the end. 'The only thing is that the reindeer are up on the roof, and I don't think they would have been able to hear that! Sing it again, please, and this time make sure it's loud enough for them to hear!'

They sang again, lustily this time. 'Well,' Father Christmas said when they'd finished, 'I'm sure that will have done the trick. Now I must say goodbye to you, and get back home to the North Pole. But there's just one thing – it's no good looking out of the window to watch me and the reindeer flying off, because as soon as they start flying, they become invisible, and so do I! So, goodbye, children, and a very happy Christmas to you all!'

Mrs Schofield opened the door and Wilf went out, accompanied by shouts of 'Thank you! Happy Christmas!' from fourteen very happy children.

'That was fantastic!' said Mrs Schofield as she escorted him upstairs. 'But I expect you've been doing it for years…'

Wilf thanked her for the compliment, resisting the temptation to tell her that it was the first time he'd played out the scene to any audience other than his little dog.

'I've got a little thank you present for Father Christmas too,' she said, offering him a packet whose shape made it obvious that it contained a bottle. Wilf thanked her, changed back into his everyday clothes, let himself quietly out of the front door and made his way home. On arrival he opened his present, and found it was a bottle of Scotch whisky.

'Right, look at that, Boots!' he said happily. 'I think I'll save that for Christmas Day and share it with Ernie!'

On Monday morning Wilf heard a knock on his door. He went to see who it was, and found Sheila standing on the doorstep. He showed her in, invited her to sit down and asked her if she would like a cup of tea, which she declined. 'I had to come round as soon as I could, Wilf,' she said, 'because I've just had a very lengthy phone call from Mrs Schofield, the lady whose house you went to on Saturday.'

'Oh dear,' Wilf replied, 'that doesn't sound too good! Did she think I wasn't good enough? I suppose she wants her money back, does she?'

Sheila laughed. 'Oh no, Wilf, nothing like that! How did you get that idea? No, on the contrary, she was absolutely delighted. She thought you were very professional, and you were very popular with the children, which of course is the important thing. And then she went through each and every detail of your routine – she was on the phone for half an hour! – I had to agree. Either you'd put a lot of work into preparing it, or else you're a natural!'

'Well, I suppose I have worked on it a bit,' Wilf replied, 'and little Boots here has had loads of Christmas presents over the past few weeks – the only thing is he still isn't very good at singing *Jingle Bells!*'

'Yes, Mrs Schofield told me about *Jingle Bells* – that was a stroke of genius, Wilf, it really was! The idea of reindeer eating children's songs to give them enough energy to get back to the North Pole… where on earth did that idea come from? It's brilliant!'

'I don't know where it came from,' said Wilf bashfully. 'I spend a lot of time on my own these days, and I think about things a lot, and sometimes ideas like that just come. So Mrs Schofield was pleased, was she?'

'You can say that again! She was so pleased she wants you to come back again next year for David's younger sister's party! She couldn't believe it when I told her it was the first time you'd done it! I've had satisfied customers on the phone before, but never anything quite like that – it was wonderful! Thank you!'

Once Sheila had gone, Wilf said to Boots, 'Right, Boots – time for a nice walk for you, I think! Would you like to go to the Forest?'

Boots wagged his tail, which Wilf interpreted as signifying approval of his suggestion.

The following Thursday evening Wilf and Ernie met for their weekly get-together at the Carlton. Once they were seated in their usual place, with their usual drinks, Ernie began their conversation with the usual question: 'So what have you been up to this last week, Wilf?'

Wilf was on the verge of giving his usual answer too: 'Not a lot', but he changed his mind and paused after the word 'Not'. 'No,' he said, 'I was going to say not a lot, because that's what I always say, but in fact quite a lot's happened. I've started a new job…'

'A new what?' Ernie exclaimed in disbelief.

'A new job.'

'That's what I thought you said. But you've retired, haven't you?'

'Yes, I retired a long time ago from Boots.'

'That's what I thought. So what do you want to go and get yourself a new job for? Haven't you got enough to do, or are you hard up?'

Wilf laughed. 'No,' he replied, 'neither of those things! In any case, it isn't a full-time job – I wouldn't like to go back to working full-time – and it's not all the year round either.'

'So what's the job?'

'I'm playing Father Christmas.'

'You're what?'

'I'm playing Father Christmas.'

'What… Do you mean in a shop?'

'No. In people's houses. People are hiring me to go to their kids' parties dressed as Father Christmas, then I chat to the kids, give them presents and so on.'

'And they pay you to do that?'

'Yes – not bad pay either!'

'Have you ever done that sort of thing before?'

'No, never.'

'So how did you know you'd be any good at it?'

'I didn't – not at first anyway. But last Saturday I had my first kids' party…'

'How did it go?'

'Well, I was very nervous when I first landed the job, but I did lots of practising at home, and then, when it came to it, I really enjoyed it, the kids enjoyed it, and the little lad's mother wants me to go back next year. So I can't be bad at doing it, can I?'

'So how many parties are you going to do?'

'I've got another three or four lined up – obviously I won't be asked to do an awful lot because people only have Christmas parties in December. Well, there may be one or two in January, but I haven't heard about any as yet.'

'Good for you, Wilf! And you say you enjoyed it?'

'Yes, I did. I just enjoyed every minute of seeing those little kids' faces and hearing them sing.'

'They sang?'

'Yes, they sang *Jingle Bells*.' Wilf went on to tell Ernie all about his routine, and how he made up his story about the reindeer needing the children's song to make them fly, and his friend listened open-mouthed.

'Well done, my friend, that's all I can say. I know I couldn't do anything like that…'

'You could, of course you could!'

'No, no way!'

'If I can do it I'm sure you could!'

'No way!'

'Why not?'

'Have you ever seen a black Father Christmas?' Ernie burst out laughing at the thought, and then Wilf joined in too. 'Oh, I've just thought of something else I haven't told you…'

'What's that?'

'Well, the lady who was running the party gave me a bottle of Scotch too, and I thought I'd save it for Christmas Day and share it with you.'

'Wow, that's really great, Wilf, thank you! What a good mate you are!'

A Happy Christmas

Two days later, it was time for Wilf's second appearance as Father Christmas, this time at a church hall in Beaconsfield Street, Hyson Green. The location of the venue meant that it was within fairly easy walking distance of his home, being not very far from Wilf and Ernie's regular drinking place, the Carlton, and not more than a hundred yards or so from Ernie's house in Burford Road. This time, however, getting into the building without being seen by the children was likely to be more difficult, because there were no upstairs rooms at all, and no cloakrooms that would not be in fairly regular use by the children. So it was arranged that somebody would meet him in the street outside the hall, and then take him down the side of the hall and admit him by way of a little-used door which would give access to a small room which served now and then as a dressing room for stage performances, and Father Christmas's entrance would be via the stage, which, it was felt, could be rather dramatic.

Wilf arrived at the appointed time, and was met outside the hall by a rather agitated lady, who told him that they had been unable to open the side-door which they were intended to use, but that they had managed to arrange for him to change into his costume in a house next door to the hall, which meant that he would have to make his entrance through the main door of the hall. The lady, Mrs Hobson, was particularly concerned, because it would mean Father Christmas might actually be seen by the general public, and she was afraid Wilf might object. Wilf hastily assured her that it made absolutely no difference to him, but she continued to fret, and Wilf was quite relieved when he eventually found himself alone and able to compose himself in the privacy of an upstairs bedroom.

Wilf deliberately remained in the bedroom until precisely two minutes before Father Christmas was due to make his appearance, the better to avoid being affected by Mrs Hobson's undue nervousness; when he eventually arrived downstairs he found that she was still fussing, terrified this time that they were going to be late. When Wilf indicated to her that he was ready to go, she half-opened the front door, peeping round it first to make sure they would not be seen, before finally opening it wide and telling him that the coast was clear. Wilf strode out confidently, ignoring her from that moment on, and not caring a jot whether he was spotted by anyone or not.

As he made his way through the outer door he could hear a raucous din emanating from the hall: laughter, screeching, shouting, excited babbling – a veritable babel of sound. Mrs Hobson prepared to open the inner door for him to make his entrance, but she hesitated because of the noise the children were making. 'Oh dear,' she worried, 'how on earth are you going to make yourself heard when you go in, with all this noise going on?'

'With this!' said Wilf, showing her a large handbell of the type that was used at one time to summon schoolchildren back to their classes after playtime.

'Clang! Clang! Clang! Clang!' went the bell. 'Happy Christmas!' yelled Wilf as loud as he could, and he strode into the middle of the floor. It was at that moment that he realised that Mrs Hobson in her nervousness had forgotten to give him the children's presents; it also occurred to him that the fault was not entirely hers, for he should have been aware enough to have reminded her. It was therefore time for some quick thinking.

'A happy Christmas, boys and girls!' Wilf said, projecting his voice so that everyone could hear. 'Are you having a good party?'

A handful of children mumbled 'yes', but most of them said nothing.

'I can't hear you!' Wilf shouted. 'I said, are you having a good party?'

This time there was much more volume in their response, but among the cries of 'Yes!', Wilf detected a couple of loud yells of 'No!', whose origin he was quick to detect.

'Now,' he went on, 'I've got a present for each of you, but…' – he deliberately started speaking more softly – 'I'll tell you a secret.'

A general hubbub ensued. 'Sssh!' said Wilf – and there was silence. 'Well,' he continued, still speaking in a quiet voice, 'as you know, I'm a very old man indeed, and I'm not as strong as I used to be. And the sack of presents for this party was too heavy for me to carry on my own, so I'm going to need a couple of really strong young boys to carry it in for me. There are two young men over here who will do just fine!' He immediately strode in the direction of the two boys whom he had heard saying they weren't having a good party, and grabbed each of them by the arm. 'I want you two fine young men to go with Mrs Hobson over here, and she will give you the sack to bring in. Off you go!'

The two boys were too much taken off their guard to protest, and they followed Mrs Hobson meekly. While they were gone, Wilf started the rest of the children singing *The First Nowell*, and then Mrs Hobson and the two boys reappeared with the missing sack.

'Thank you,' said Wilf, 'I couldn't have managed without you! Now tell me your names.'

'Roy,' said one.

'Keith,' said the other.

'Right then, Roy and Keith, you've been so helpful that I really think you deserve to get your presents first. Here you are, Roy,' he said, pulling a packet from the sack and giving it to him, then repeating his actions for Keith. 'Okay, now everyone, I want you to give three hearty cheers for my little helpers Roy and Keith! Hip-hip-hip…'

'Hooray!' all cried with enthusiasm – and again and again until the ritual of the three cheers was complete.

By this time Roy and Keith had recovered from their embarrassment, but Wilf had won them over, and they stood opening their presents as eagerly as anyone else there. When all the presents were gone, Wilf began the same routine with which he had closed the proceedings at the previous party, ending with an enthusiastic rendering of *Jingle Bells*, in which Wilf was delighted to note, Roy and Keith joined as lustily as anyone. The song over, Wilf left the hall noisily clanging his bell as he went. Mrs Hobson accompanied him and, two minutes later, she and Wilf were once more back in the house next door.

'I think you were wonderful,' Mrs Hobson said, as soon as they stepped inside. 'I was so worried about those two boys you picked out, because I know how troublesome they can be. And at the end you had them eating out of your hand! How on earth did you do it?'

'Ho! Ho! Ho! It's the magic of Father Christmas!' replied Wilf, after which he went upstairs to change, then took his leave of the no longer nervous Mrs Hobson, and made his way home.

The next day Wilf was in action again, for this was the day of the party to which Sheila had promised to drive him, because it would have been quite complicated for him to get there without a car, and in any case the hostess was a friend of hers. She turned up at 3.30 as she had arranged, and as soon as Wilf got in the car alongside her, she started talking about the previous day's party.

'Well, Wilf,' she said, you appear to have done it again! I've had Mrs Hobson on the phone half the morning, and she couldn't stop singing your praises!'

'Oh,' replied Wilf, 'so you've heard about the two naughty little boys, I suppose.'

'Oh yes,' she chuckled. 'Poor Mrs Hobson was terrified of what they might get up to – I told her she should have told me about her worries first,'

'I'm glad she didn't, because if I'd known beforehand I don't think it would have worked.'

'Well, the important thing is that it did work, Wilf! I don't know how you did it. Have you ever been on the stage, you know, ever had any acting experience?'

'No, never,' Wilf replied.'

'And you've never been a teacher either?'

'What, me? You must be joking, Sheila! I've been a factory hand all my life!'

'Well, all the more credit to you then! By the way, I've actually been invited to stay for today's party, but I told my friend Celia I'd have to ask you first, because I wouldn't like to think I was putting you off.'

'You wouldn't put me off! The very idea!'

'How can you be so sure?'

'Because the party is for the kids, and Father Christmas is for the kids, and anybody who isn't a kid wouldn't get a look in! Once I get started I ignore all the grown-ups!'

'Quite right too!' said Sheila. 'What a professional you are!'

Wilf simply beamed with pleasure, and said no more because the car was drawing to a stop outside Celia's house in a little street just off Woodthorpe Road, and Wilf was mentally preparing himself for his next change of character.

This time nothing went wrong; in fact it was almost a repeat of Wilf's first party in West Bridgford, the only significant difference being that instead of Father Christmas receiving a bottle of Scotch as a thank you present, this time it was a bottle of French red wine – and a particularly good one, Sheila assured him during the drive home.

'You know, Wilf, every single party you've done so far, I've been inundated with calls saying how good you were, and this time I don't need anyone to tell me, because I've seen it for myself. You really are fantastic! I never imagined when I set this business up that I'd get somebody as clever and as dedicated as you to work for me. I'm so, so grateful for all the effort you put in!'

'But I don't find it an effort at all,' Wilf replied. 'If a thing's worth doing, it's worth doing well, my old Dad used to say to me, and if it's not worth doing well, it's not worth doing at all. And you know what? I can't remember the last time I felt so happy! When I look at the faces of those little kids, the wonder in their eyes and the joy in their singing, it takes away years and years of pain.'

'Even when you have kids like that pair at Mrs Hobson's do?'

'Even Roy and Keith. You know, I'm sure there probably are some evil kids around, but the moment I looked into Roy's and Keith's eyes, I knew they were all right really. They were just a little older than most of the kids there, and they were a bit embarrassed about being there, and they just felt the need to show off, that's all.'

'A psychologist as well then, Wilf! You're quite a man!'

'I don't know about that,' said Wilf modestly, although inside he felt intensely happy at hearing Sheila's words.

'Something I was just thinking about the party you're doing next weekend,' Sheila said, as they were arriving back at Wilf's house, 'is that it would probably be a good idea for me to give you a lift again.'

'No, there's no need,' said Wilf, 'it's only in Sherwood – I can get there easily.'

'But there's Sherwood and Sherwood. Yes, I know there are some parts of Sherwood you would be able to get to easily, but this party is in Victoria Crescent. Do you know where that is?'

'No, I don't,' Wilf replied. 'I haven't looked at the street map yet.'

'Well,' Sheila resumed, 'it's up at the top of Private Road.'

'Oh, I know where that is. I can get a bus to Private Road.'

'Yes, I know you can. But have you ever been up Private Road?'

Wilf confessed that he hadn't.

'Victoria Crescent is about six hundred yards up Private Road, and it's quite a steep hill, especially for a man of your age.'

'I'm all right!' Wilf insisted. 'I'm as fit as a fiddle!'

'Yes, I know – and that's how I want you to stay! So I'll come and pick you up about half past three again, okay?'

'Okay,' Wilf agreed reluctantly.

So, on the following Sunday, just eleven days before Christmas Day, Sheila called to pick up Wilf as she had promised, and, almost as soon as the car turned into Private Road, Wilf quickly understood why she had been so insistent, because the hill really was quite steep, and he recognised that it would have been difficult for him to negotiate, especially carrying the suitcase which contained his costume.

'I wonder why it's called Private Road,' Wilf said. 'It seems a very strange name for a road.'

'Yes, it does, doesn't it? Someone who once lived here told me that at one time it really was a private road which belonged to the house owners, and they used to have to maintain the road themselves, at their own expense. Then, I believe, the Council took over the maintenance of the road, but the residents still had to pay a proportion of the cost, in return for which they kept the right to restrict the flow of traffic up and down the road. That's why if we were to go further up, we'd be able to see a gate, which is often locked – all the residents have a key, you see. If we went all the way to the top we'd get to Woodborough Road, and without the gate, the residents were afraid that the road would be clogged up with cars taking a short cut through from Woodborough Road to Mansfield Road and vice versa. In fact, if we'd approached Private Road from Woodborough Road, we'd have had to go through the gate to get to Victoria Crescent, and we might have found the gate locked!'

'That gate must cause more trouble than it's worth!' Wilf exclaimed.

'I understand that's what some of the residents think too! But there's no doubt about it, without the gate the road would be an awful lot busier.'

'There are some very big houses up here...'

'Oh yes, there are some... I think originally a lot of them were built by wealthy lacemakers. Now the house we're going to in Victoria Crescent, that has quite a history. Do you know the name D. H. Lawrence?'

'The writer, you mean?'

'Yes.'

'I know the name, because there was a lot of hoo-hah a few years back about one of his books – *Lady Chatterley's Lover*, wasn't it?'

'That's right. Anyway, the house we're going to, number 32, used to belong to a professor at Nottingham University, and D. H. Lawrence ran away with his wife! Here we are, this is it!'

Wilf looked at the house, a very large Victorian villa whose front wall was covered with ivy, and the whole house surrounded by greenery. 'I don't think I've ever been in a house as big as that in my life!' he said.

'It is big, yes. It's beautiful too. But don't feel intimidated. The young couple who own it are really nice, and their daughter Emily is a real sweetie. She's only three – I think she turns four towards the end of January. I did tell you that the children at this party would be younger than at the other ones you've done, didn't I?'

'Oh yes, don't worry, I've been changing my act a bit to take account of that.'

'I don't doubt it!' said Sheila. 'I think I know you well enough by now to expect you to do your homework properly! And of course, there are only going to be eight of them there, so it won't be a scrum like the one you went to in Hyson Green!'

As they approached the house they saw the front door open; the hostess had been watching out for their arrival to avoid their having to ring the doorbell. She was a tall, attractive and beautifully dressed woman with darkish skin and with very curly dark hair, in her mid-twenties, Wilf thought to himself. 'Hello,' she said, holding out her hand, 'I'm Ruth. I'll show you upstairs so you can change.'

'And I'll be back to pick you up at about half past five, Wilf,' said Sheila.

'Okay,' Wilf replied.

'Why don't you stay?' Ruth suggested. 'By the time you get home it will be almost time to come over here again! We've got plenty of room, so stay if you like!'

'Oh, all right, if you're sure,' said Sheila.

Ruth took Wilf upstairs to a bedroom so he could change, gave him the children's presents, each bearing a label with the child's name written on it, and then went downstairs again to take Sheila into the room where the children were playing a game of 'Pass the parcel', supervised by Ruth's husband Michael, while two visiting mothers were putting the final touches to the tea-table.

'Well,' Wilf thought to himself as he stowed the parcels into his sack, 'at least I have the presents this time – but I'd better make sure Emily's is on top, so that she will be the first little girl to get her present.'

He proceeded to put on his costume – first the padding, then the scarlet trousers, then the black boots; after that came the jacket, scarlet like the trousers but trimmed with white fur, followed by a broad shiny black belt which he fastened around his now more than ample figure. All that now remained was to transform his head. He removed the glasses which he normally wore all the time, and placed them on the dressing-table alongside the wig, beard and hat he had placed there earlier. Looking in the dressing-table mirror he now donned his snow-white wig, a pair of false eyebrows, his flowing white beard and a pair of rimless spectacles which he felt were more in character than his normal pair, although he had had them specially made to the same prescription, so that he would be able to read the names on the presents he had to distribute. He reached out to pick up his red hat, again fur-trimmed and with a large white bobble on the top, but accidentally knocked his everyday glasses to the floor as he took his hat from the dressing-table. He bent down to retrieve them, but found that, although he was able to see them all right, the padding he was wearing made it quite impossible for him to bend down to reach them, so he resolved to pick them up afterwards, when he would be no longer encumbered by his bulky padding. He had just put on his hat and done a final check in the mirror to make sure all was well, when he heard a quiet tap on the door: it was Ruth, come to tell him that they were ready for him.

Ruth led him downstairs, then tapped on the door of the drawing-room. From the other side of the door he heard a man's voice shouting, 'Look, children! Look who's come to see you!' Then the door suddenly opened, and he made his appearance – rather less noisily than usual, for fear of scaring the little ones.

'Hello, children!' he said. 'Happy Christmas!'

Some of the children returned the greeting, but by no means all. 'Who knows what my name is?' he asked them.

'Father Christmas!' shouted one little boy.

'No, it's not, it's Santa Claus!' said his neighbour.

'Yes, you're both right!' said Wilf. 'Some people call me Santa Claus, some call me Father Christmas, but I don't mind which name you use, as long as you're happy to see me, and you have a nice Christmas!'

The two boys who had initially disagreed over what to call him now seemed satisfied, and Wilf could see one or two smiling faces, but the fact that one or two little ones were still clinging to their mothers had not escaped his notice.

'Now,' Wilf continued, 'you know what my name is, but I don't know yours! Now which one's Emily?'

In actual fact Wilf was already fairly certain which one was Emily, because he had noticed a pretty little girl with frizzy hair, wearing a navy blue party dress with white polka dots, and sporting a big white ribbon in her hair; what was more, she was standing very close to Ruth. Sure enough, the little girl he had spotted put up her hand; Wilf, now in full Father Christmas mode, stepped forward, said, 'Hello, Emily, how nice to meet you!' He then took her hand and raised it to his lips, saying, 'And what a pretty little girl you are!' Then he shook Emily's mother's hand and turned his attention to the others: he asked each child their name, kissed the hands of all the little girls and shook the hands of all the little boys. Having spoken to all of them, he then returned to his original position.

'Now then,' he announced, 'I have presents for all of you! So when I call your name I want you to come and see me – and bring your Mummy as well if you like – and then I'll give you your present.' He reached into his sack and took out the first present. 'And the first present is for Emily!' he called, turning towards the little girl in the blue spotted dress.

Emily came up to him, accompanied by her mother who, after Father Christmas had given Emily her present, said to her daughter, 'What do you say to Father Christmas, Emily?'

'Thank you, Father Christmas!' said Emily dutifully and, before turning away, she looked up into his eyes, smiled and said shyly, 'I love you, Father Christmas!'

'And I love you too, Emily,' said Wilf.

After Emily had returned to her place Wilf gave presents to all the other children, correctly identifying every single one of them and leaving each of them delighted that Father Christmas had remembered their name.

Once the sack was empty Wilf said to them all, 'Well, it's time for me to go, I'm afraid. Now I'm sure you know that I ride in a sleigh, don't you?'

'Yes!' they chorused, in a way that showed they were no longer the shy, vaguely suspicious individuals they had seemed at first.

'And what do I have to pull my sleigh?'

'Reindeer!' shouted one little boy.

'Yes! And do you know the name of any of my reindeer?'

Three of the children answered this time: 'Rudolph!'

'And do any of you know what Rudolph has?'

'A very shiny nose!' they shouted as one.

'That reminds me of a song,' said Wilf. 'I'll sing it, and if you know it, you sing it with me!'

Then he began to sing and, after not more than three or four words of the song, every voice in the room was singing:

Tony Whelpton

Rudolph the red-nosed reindeer,
Had a very shiny nose,
And if you ever saw it,
You would even say it glows…

At the end of the song, Wilf said, 'Now I'm afraid it's time for me to go, children. Goodbye, everyone, and a very, very happy Christmas!'

With that he left the room, went back upstairs to the bedroom to change, and, as he got into Sheila's car prior to returning home, the cheers of the children were still ringing in his ears.

'Wilf,' said Sheila as they drove off, 'do you know what Ruth, the hostess, said to me just now?'

'I have no idea,' answered Wilf. 'Didn't she think I was good enough?'

'Don't be ridiculous! No, I'll tell you what she said, because you'd never imagine anyone saying this sort of thing to you. She said, "You know, that man's an absolute genius! How on earth did he manage to learn all the children's names so quickly! And the way he related to them – it was incredible. They all loved him to bits. And promise me you'll tell him exactly what I said." So what about that then?'

'Oh, it was nothing really, just that I saw that some of them were a bit shy and needed to be treated gently, and I've always had a good memory, so I made a point of memorising their names as soon as I heard them. It's a good job there were only eight of them, mind, or I might have had more difficulty!'

'Well, it was an absolutely outstanding performance! I can see I shall have to give you a pay rise if I want you to do it again next year!'

'No,' said Wilf, 'that won't be necessary! I've had such a good time, I'd happily do it again for nothing!'

'I wouldn't dream of not paying you! You're a professional! You know, when I watch you there interacting with those children, I can't help thinking too that you're a born grandad! It's so sad you've never had grandchildren of your own...'

'Well, that's what I used to think too, but thanks to you, I now feel that I do have some of my own!'

By that time the car had arrived at Wilf's house, and Wilf and Sheila said their goodbyes, with Sheila saying she would pop in to see him just before Christmas.

It was not until Wilf was getting undressed for bed that night that he suddenly realised as he was taking off his glasses, that they were his Father Christmas ones. 'That's odd,' he said to Boots, 'I wonder where I left the others! They must be in the suitcase with my costume, I suppose. Oh well, I'll have a look in the morning – I won't need them in the night.' But in the middle of the night he suddenly woke up, and remembered knocking his glasses off the dressing-table at Ruth's house, and not being able to retrieve them. 'I am an idiot!' he scolded himself. 'How on earth did I forget to pick them up when I changed out of my costume? And there I was, boasting to Sheila about having a good memory!'

The following morning Wilf took Boots out for his morning walk, and chose to take him to the Forest via Leslie Road, so that he could call in and tell Sheila about his missing glasses. He rang her doorbell.

'Wilf!' Sheila said as soon as she saw him, 'I'm glad you've come! Have you lost a pair of glasses, by any chance?'

'Yes, I have,' he replied, 'and that's why I've come to see you. I realised that I must have left them in the room where I changed before the party yesterday, and I wondered if you could ring Ruth and ask her to put them in the post for me?'

'There's no need,' she assured him. 'I had a phone call from Ruth half an hour ago, and she's going to drop them off at your house this afternoon.'

'Oh, that's very kind of her! How did she know they were mine?'

'Because they couldn't possibly be anybody else's! She says she found them under the dressing-table in the room where you'd been changing, and they were obviously men's glasses. Now they've only been living in that house for a couple of months, and the only man apart from you who's been in the house since then is her husband Michael, and Michael doesn't wear glasses, so they must have been yours. Easy!'

That afternoon, at about five minutes before four o'clock, Wilf put the kettle on to make himself a cup of tea, as he always did at that time of day. He was just removing the tea caddy from its shelf when he heard a knock at the door. He put back the tea caddy and went to open the door. It was Ruth.

'Hello, Wilf, I've come to give you your glasses back!' said Ruth.

'It's very kind of you to bring them over,' said Wilf. 'I'm sorry to cause you all this trouble…'

'Not at all,' she replied, 'it's no trouble! And in any case, I'm glad of having the opportunity to come and say thank you for all you did yesterday.'

'Well, come in then,' said Wilf.

'Okay,' Ruth replied, 'just for a couple of minutes – I've got so much to do at home, with Christmas coming up!'

So Wilf led her into his living-room and they both sat down.

'You know,' said Ruth, 'you were such a hit with the children yesterday! And especially with Emily – she couldn't stop talking about you! You know what she said?'

Wilf didn't know, but Ruth was going to tell him anyway.

'She said – no, she kept on saying over and over again – I love Father Christmas! I wish I could have him for my grandad! Because Emily doesn't have any grandads, you see… It was so sweet!'

'She's a very sweet girl,' said Wilf. He was just about to say that he wished she were his granddaughter too, but, feeling it would perhaps not be appropriate, and feeling tears welling into his eyes, he said instead, 'Can I get you a cup of tea? The kettle's just boiled, and I always have one myself at this time.'

'Oh, all right then, if you're having one anyway...'

So Wilf retired to the kitchen to make the tea. When he returned, he found Ruth standing by the fire-place, holding in her hand the old photograph of Wilf's daughter Susan eating an ice cream on Mablethorpe beach. She looked up at him, and said: 'Wilf, a funny question – but why have you got a picture of my Mum on your mantelpiece?'

Wilf looked at Ruth, but said nothing for a moment: his head was in a whirl, and he needed to sit down. He stumbled into an armchair, but his head was still spinning. Ruth came over to him quickly and said, 'Wilf, are you all right?'

Wilf looked up at her. 'Yes, I think so,' he said. 'I don't know what happened. I just came over all peculiar – I thought I was going to faint.'

'Can I get you something? A glass of water?'

'No, thanks, I think I shall be all right now I'm sitting down. The tea will sort me out. Oh dear, I don't know what came over me...'

'You just had a funny turn, that's all – has that sort of thing happened to you before?'

'No, never. I don't know what happened... I remember you said something to me, and then my head suddenly started going round and round and my legs turned to jelly... I can't remember what it was you said – something about a photograph... Oh, never mind, it must have been my mind playing tricks, I suppose...'

Ruth looked down at her hands, in which she was still holding the photograph; yes, there was no mistake, it was the same photograph all right. Then she looked at Wilf again, and instead of the sprightly, cheerful character who had played Father Christmas so effectively, she saw now a vulnerable, shaking old man. I must be careful, she told herself, I don't know what's going on, but it looks as if the question I asked him gave him a nasty turn. 'I did say something about a photograph, that's right,' she said at last. 'While you were in the kitchen making the tea I was looking at this photo. And I was wondering – Wilf, who's this little girl?'

Wilf looked at the photo she was holding, and immediately said, 'Oh, that's Susan. It was taken on the beach at Mablethorpe just after I came home from the army. It must have been 1946, I suppose...'

'Susan? Who was Susan?'

'She was my little girl.'

'You mean your daughter?'

'Yes, that's right.'

'Where is she now?'

'I wish I knew... I haven't seen her for nearly thirty years.'

'Why?'

'Oh, it was one of those family fall-outs. Cissy... Oh, you didn't know Cissy, did you? Cissy was my wife... Cissy didn't like Susan's choice of boyfriend.'

'Why not?'

'Because he was black.'

'Black?'

'Yes, he came from Jamaica, and Cissy didn't think it was right for a white girl to go with a black boy.'

'What did you think?'

'I was worried about it a bit, but mostly because of any children they might have if they got married.'

'What do you mean?'

'Well, there was a lot of bad feeling in Nottingham at that time between whites and blacks, and I was worried that any children they might have would get rejected by both sides. Cissy and I had lots of rows about it for years, even after Susan upped and left...'

'Susan ran away from home?'

'Yes, and we never saw her again.'

Ruth observed Wilf's trembling voice and the tears which were beginning to fill his eyes.

'So... what was the name of Susan's boyfriend?

'Courtney – Courtney Reid.'

Ruth walked across to where Wilf was sitting, took his hands in hers and suddenly fell to her knees. 'What are you doing?' Wilf asked.

It was a minute or two before Ruth was able to answer, for a lump had come into her throat and tears were running down her face.

'Oh, Wilf,' she said at last. 'Oh, Wilf...'

'What's the matter? Why are you crying?'

'Because I'm sad and happy at the same time.'

'Why?'

'Oh, Wilf,' she said again, looking up into his eyes. 'Because Susan and Courtney were my Mum and Dad, and that means I'm your granddaughter, and I couldn't wish for a more wonderful grandad!'

'What do you mean? I don't understand what you're saying...'

Ruth stood up again and took Wilf's hands in hers once more. 'As you know, my name's Ruth Elliott. But before I married Michael Elliott my name was Ruth Reid, and my Mum and Dad were Susan and Courtney Reid. And I recognised the photograph of my Mum as a little girl because I've got the very same photograph at home – I'll show you when you come and see us. I've been looking at it only recently, so there's no mistake. And that means you're my grandad! Oh, you've no idea how happy that makes me – I always wanted to have a grandad, just like the other kids!'

'I can't believe this!' Wilf said, getting to his feet. 'So you're my Susan's little girl...'

'Yes! And that means I'm your granddaughter! Look,' she said, doing a twirl in front of Wilf. Then, dropping into a curtsey, she continued, 'So what do you think?'

'Beautiful!' he exclaimed, 'it's beautiful and you're beautiful... And that means Emily is...'

'Your great-granddaughter! And she's already told you she loves you, hasn't she!'

'Oh yes, of course she has – that made my day, that did! And now it makes me feel even happier! So – what

117

about Susan and Courtney – are they in Nottingham too?'

'No, I'm afraid they're not. But I'll tell you about them in a little while – I've just noticed the time, and I must be getting home. Would you like to come with me?'

'What, now?'

'Yes, of course…'

'But what about Boots?'

'Boots?'

'My dog.'

'Oh, bring him too – but you'd better bring something for him to eat though. We've got a pretty well-stocked larder, but I don't think it runs to dog food! Emily will be delighted to meet Boots – she loves dogs.'

'No,' said Wilf, after a moment's thought. 'I don't think that's a good idea – Emily's going to have enough new things to cope with when we get back to your place and start re-arranging her life! I'll put some food down for Boots before we go and then we can leave him here. There'll be plenty of opportunity for her to get to know him once the novelty of having a new great-grandad has worn off!'

'Perhaps you're right,' said Ruth. 'If you're sure he'll be okay.'

'He'll be as right as rain,' said Wilf. 'But I've just had another thought about Emily…'

'What's that?' 'Well, Emily thinks I'm Father Christmas, doesn't she? How's she going to feel when she finds out that it wasn't Father Christmas at all, it was just an old man dressed up? The magic of Christmas would all be shattered for her, wouldn't it!'

'Oh, Wilf,' Ruth said with a smile. 'Just think. Okay, she might lose the illusion that Father Christmas is real, I grant you that, but that's an illusion that will be lost one day anyway. Weigh against that the fact that she's gaining a grandfather, when she's always thought that she'd never have one. And add to that the fact that she told me she wished she could have you as her grandad – oh, Wilf! – that's where the real magic comes in!'

'Well yes, of course,' replied Wilf. 'There's only one thing wrong with that...'

'Oh? What?'

'She's not gaining a grandfather – she's gaining a great-grandfather! You're the one that's gaining a grandfather!'

'I know, and I couldn't be more delighted either!'

Wilf and Ruth fell into each other's arms, tears of happiness streaming down both of their faces; it was an embrace which lasted several minutes, as Wilf felt years of unhappiness and solitude evaporating from the deep recesses of his heart. Ten minutes later, Wilf, Boots and Ruth were driving towards Victoria Crescent to break the news to Emily and Michael.

Ruth parked her BMW in the drive and led Wilf into the house, where they found Michael in the kitchen. 'Oh,' Ruth said, 'where's Emily?'

'She's in the playroom,' her husband answered, looking quizzically at Wilf.

'Oh, okay,' Ruth replied, then, indicating Wilf, 'you remember Wilf, don't you?'

'No,' Michael answered, 'I don't think I've had the pleasure.'

'But he was here only yesterday!' Then, suddenly remembering, she added, 'Sorry, I was forgetting, you only met him when he was dressed as Father Christmas! Michael, this is Wilf.'

Michael shook Wilf by the hand and said, 'Pleased to meet you, Wilf. That was a great job you did yesterday – thank you!'

Wilf beamed, and Ruth resumed, 'There's something you don't know, Michael – in fact I've only found out this afternoon myself. You know that my mother was born in Nottingham and only went to London just before she and Dad got married...'

'Yes?'

'Well, would you believe it – I've found out this afternoon that Wilf is actually my Mum's Dad, so Michael, meet your new grandfather-in-law!'

The look on Michael's face changed in an instant from one of puzzlement to one of sheer delight, and he stepped forward to shake Wilf's hand once more, though much more warmly this time.

'And now,' Ruth continued, 'we'd better go to the playroom and introduce Emily to her great-grandad!'

The three of them went into another room where Emily was sitting on the floor surrounded by toys;

totally absorbed by what she was doing, she did not even look up.

'Emily, there's a visitor come to see you!' said Ruth. 'Do you know who this is?'

Emily looked up, shook her head, and turned her attention back to her toys.

'You remember Father Christmas came to your party yesterday, don't you? Well, this is Father Christmas!'

'He doesn't look like Father Christmas,' Emily complained.

'That's because I haven't got my reindeer with me today,' said Wilf, putting on his Father Christmas voice.

At once Emily recognised his voice and began to move towards him, but then she hesitated and, her own voice tinged with disappointment, said, 'Why?'

'We've got something very special to tell you, Emily,' said Ruth. 'Shall I tell her, Wilf, or would you like to?'

'I think I'd like to if you don't mind, because I think I've got some explaining to do,' said Wilf. 'Emily, will you come and sit on my knee like you did the other day when you told me you loved me and I told you I loved you too...'

'Yes,' she answered, and once she was settled on his knee, Wilf began his explanation.

'Now,' he said, 'I want you to tell me, Emily, have you ever met Father Christmas?'

Emily looked puzzled once more. 'Oh yes,' she said, 'I saw him when he came to my party, and I saw him when Mummy took me shopping in Griffin and Spalding's.'

'Ah,' said Wilf mysteriously, 'then that means you haven't seen Father Christmas at all. You see, the real Father Christmas only comes on Christmas Eve, and the Father Christmases you see at parties and in shops are pretend Father Christmases...'

'You mean the Father Christmas that came to my party was just you dressed up?'

'Yes, that's right. The real Father Christmas is far too busy getting ready for Christmas Eve to go to everybody's party!'

'But there's something else to tell you,' said Ruth. 'You know I've always told you that I didn't have a grandad...'

'Yes,' Emily replied, wondering where this was leading.

'Well, I only thought I didn't have one, because my Mummy didn't know where he was. And I've just found out that I had one all the time, and he was living in Nottingham. So this,' she said, indicating Wilf, 'is my grandad, and if he's my grandad, that means he's your great-grandad! And now we've found him, we're not going to let him go! Are we, Grandad?'

'No fear, we're not!' Wilf confirmed. 'Not now I've found out that I've got the prettiest great-granddaughter in the world!'

Just then another thought suddenly came into Wilf's mind, and he continued talking, addressing his remarks now to Ruth as well, whilst ostensibly still talking to Emily.

'Your Mummy said that her Mummy didn't know where her Daddy was. So I've got a question to ask her...'

'Yes?' answered Ruth.

'I suppose your Dad didn't know where his Dad was either, did he?'

'No, that's right, he didn't.'

'Do you know what his name was?'

'Courtney.'

'No, your Dad's name was Courtney. I mean the name of Courtney's Dad...'

'Oh, I see... I seem to remember his name was Ernest.'

'That's right. Now then... What would you say if I told you that Ernest Reid is my best friend, and I meet him every Thursday evening for a drink?'

'What! You must be joking!'

'No, I wouldn't joke about something like that! I've only recently met him, and he'd been looking for me for years! And he lives not very far from me, what's more!'

'So that means I've found two long-lost grandads in one day! That's amazing!'

'Even more amazing for Emily!' Michael pointed out. 'She's found two long-lost great-grandads in one day!'

'And what about me?' said Wilf. 'I've found a granddaughter I didn't know I had, I've found a grandson-in law, and there's a pretty little girl who's told me already that she loves me, and she turns out to be my great-granddaughter! That's unbelievable, and it makes me so happy!'

'I know,' said Ruth, 'but it's a bit special too, for all of us.'

'So tell me about Susan and Courtney,' said Wilf.

Ruth and Michael exchanged glances, and then Ruth answered, 'We will, but not until the little one's in bed. Now I'd better see about getting us some supper – you must be starving, Wilf… er, Grandad…'

'You know, Ruth, hearing you call me Grandad is just about the nicest thing I've heard in years!'

'Well, look, you and Michael can get Emily ready for bed, and I'll start cooking. Then perhaps Great-grandad would like to read Emily her bedtime story tonight…'

So Ruth withdrew to the kitchen and Wilf and Michael went up to Emily's bedroom, where Emily immediately made for her bookshelf and pulled out a book which she handed to Wilf. 'Please will you read this one?' she asked.

'Of course I will,' said Wilf.

'But first it's bath time!' said Michael. 'Great-grandad will read to you after that…'

'Oh, Daddy, that's not fair!' Emily complained.

'Yes, it is! Come on, you little monkey! We'll leave Great-grandad to look at the book and then we'll be really quick, okay?'

'Okay, Daddy,' she answered somewhat reluctantly – although she then proceeded to make for the bathroom as fast as she could.

Once she had gone, leaving him sitting on a chair beside Emily's empty bed, Wilf looked at the book she had handed to him. On the cover was a picture of Father Christmas bearing a sack full of presents, just about to enter a room where a little girl was asleep in bed. The name of the book was *Twas The Night Before Christmas*. Wilf smiled and opened the book, with which he was familiar, for his own father had read it to him when he was a little boy – it had been written ninety years before Wilf had been born. He flicked through the pages looking at the pictures on every page, for he found the words had lost none of their familiarity – or their magic – in the intervening years.

In no time at all Michael and Emily returned. 'Mmm! You smell nice!' said Wilf.

'Right – into bed!' Michael ordered.

'Oh Daddy! Can I sit on Great-grandad's knee?'

'Oh, all right, if you want to,' said Wilf. 'Hop up then!'

'Goodnight kiss for me first!' Michael demanded, and once his wish had been granted he went back downstairs, leaving Emily with her new great-grandad; she climbed upon his knee, put her arms round his neck and gave him a big kiss on the cheek.

'Oh, Great-grandad, I'm so happy!' she said. 'I'm so glad we found you!'

'So am I,' Wilf replied, and then he began to read the familiar words of Clement Clarke Moore's poem:

'Twas the night before Christmas, when all through the house
Not a creature was stirring, not even a mouse.
The stockings were hung by the chimney with care,
In hopes that St Nicholas soon would be there.'

Once the story was over, Emily climbed down from Wilf's knee and jumped into bed. Wilf tucked her in snugly, she kissed him on the cheek once more and then whispered in his ear. Only then did she say good night, closed her eyes and smiled.

'Good night, little angel,' said Wilf, after which he switched off the light, closed the bedroom door and made his way downstairs, with tears streaming down his face.

'Wilf!' said Ruth, the moment she saw him. 'What's wrong? Why are you crying?'

'It's that dear little girl of yours,' he said. 'Do you know what she just said to me?'

'Tell me…'

'All she said was, "Goodnight, Great-grandfather Christmas!" and I just couldn't stop the tears coming. You've no idea how happy I am, Ruth…'

'I have, Grandad,' said Ruth, 'because I feel exactly the same.'

When Michael came back into the kitchen he found Ruth in Wilf's arms; both of them were crying their eyes out.

'Well,' he exclaimed. 'I thought this was an occasion to celebrate. But obviously I was wrong, so I'd better put this back in the cellar…'

Only then did Wilf and Ruth look up and see the bottle of champagne he was holding. 'No!' shouted Ruth. 'Don't you dare! We've stopped crying now!'

'Yes,' said Wilf, brushing away the remaining tears. 'We'll manage somehow…'

All three of them laughed, Michael opened the champagne and they each drank to their new-found family; after taking a few sips from her glass Ruth returned to the kitchen to continue preparing supper, leaving Wilf alone with Michael.

'So how long have you been living in Nottingham, Michael?' asked Wilf.

'Oh, just over two months now.'

'Do you like it?'

'Oh yes, very much indeed – and especially the house. We couldn't have afforded a place like this in London. We've got an enormous garden – it's going to be lovely for Emily having this amount of space!'

'Is that why you decided to come back to Nottingham?'

'No, but when the offer came of a new job for both of us, it made it a lot easier.'

'So what do you do?'

'We're both lawyers. Well, Ruth is the real lawyer, because she's actually practising. I just talk about it – I'm a lecturer in Law at the university. But Ruth will have to have some time off work fairly soon, because Emily's going to have a little brother or sister...'

'Oh, that's wonderful! She didn't tell me that...'

'Well, I expect there's going to be a lot that you'll need to tell each other about!'

'Of course there is! And apart from anything else, I'm looking forward to being able to make things up with Susan, Ruth's Mum. It's been far too long... And of course it's too late for Cissy, my wife, to make her peace with Susan, because Cissy died last year, but that doesn't mean I can't.'

Just at that moment Ruth appeared with the food. 'You can't do what, Wilf?' she asked.

'I was just saying that it's a long time since Cissy and I fell out with your Mum, and it's too late for Cissy to patch things up because she died last year, but that doesn't mean it's too late for me...'

'Oh, I see... Well, er...' Ruth put the plates on the table, then went over to Wilf, put her arms around his neck and then continued, 'Oh, there's no easy way to say this, Wilf, but I'm afraid it's too late for you too...'

'I don't know what you mean...'

'I mean that Susan and Courtney died even before Cissy did.'

'What?'

'I'm sorry, Grandad, we weren't able to let you know because we didn't know where you were – we didn't even know you were still alive. My Mum and Dad lived in Lewisham, and they'd been over to visit us in Clapham, only a few weeks after Emily was born. They were driving back home along Peckham High Street, and some young idiot who had had too much to drink lost control of his car and smashed into them. The best you can say is that they didn't feel a thing. They both died instantly. I'm sorry…'

'There's no need for you to be sorry, Ruth! I'm sorry that I didn't do more to stop things getting out of hand!'

'But if you had, perhaps Michael and I wouldn't have met, and Emily wouldn't even have been born…'

'Yes,' said Wilf, 'we can't turn the clock back, can we… What I can't understand is why I'm not crying over the news that Susan is dead. I suppose the truth is that I did all my grieving many years ago. The Lord knows I've cried about her enough over the years… But it must have been awful for you.'

'Yes, it was, and one of the really bad things was that Emily lost one set of grandparents before she'd even been able to start getting to know them. And Michael's parents both died when he was little, so that was the end of Emily's grandparents!'

'But at least now she's got great-grandparents she didn't know about,' Michael interjected.

'Well, yes,' said Ruth, 'that's true. But let's eat before this food gets too cold. We've still got a lot to tell each other, and I expect there will be a few more tears to shed yet, so we need to keep our strength up!'

So they all took their seats at the dining-table and began to eat. There was so much for the three of them to talk about that the meal Ruth had prepared did not receive the credit it deserved, but the events of the day had been so momentous that nothing was further from Ruth's mind than what they were eating. First of all Ruth told Wilf as much as she knew about Susan and Courtney's arrival in London, their initial stay in Brixton, their employment at County Hall, and their subsequent move to Lewisham when they had learned that Susan was pregnant with Ruth. Wilf then told them of his abortive attempts to discover where Susan and Courtney were, and the story Courtney's father had told him about his own efforts.

Suddenly Ruth gasped. 'Oh God!' she cried. 'How could I be so stupid! I should have thought of that before! Excuse me, I just need to fetch something from the study – I shan't be a minute!' With that, she rushed out of the room.

'I'm sorry, Wilf,' said Michael. 'I can't imagine what she's up to! Let's have another glass of wine while she's fetching whatever it is she's looking for!'

Without waiting for Wilf to reply, Michael picked up the bottle and filled both their glasses, but before he had time to sit down again Ruth reappeared carrying a tin box which bore the words 'Quality Street'. She removed the lid from the tin and Wilf saw that it contained a lot of photographs; Ruth rummaged through it and finally, with a cry of triumph, she held out a photo for Wilf to see. 'Here you are, Wilf, I can't imagine why I didn't think of this before! Is there anybody in this photo you recognise?'

Wilf reached out, took the photo, and as soon as he saw it, he gasped. 'Oh, yes!' he cried. 'Too right I do! That's my Susan! And the chap that's with her, that must be Courtney, I suppose...'

'That's right, it is,' Ruth confirmed. 'And that was taken on their wedding day! I remember my Mum telling me that they got married at Lewisham Registry Office, and nobody else but the Registrar was there, because they didn't know anybody well enough to invite them!'

'But they must have had witnesses!' Michael objected. 'A marriage isn't legal unless there are two witnesses!'

'The witnesses were two people who worked in the Registry Office,' said Ruth. 'The Registrar asked them who their witnesses were, and when they said they didn't have anybody, he sent somebody out to find some, and their witnesses were a switchboard operator and a porter! And then afterwards, they went into some gardens on the other side of Lewisham High Street from the Registry Office, and asked someone to take a photo of them on a little Brownie box camera that Courtney had!'

'Well, well,' Wilf exclaimed. 'What a lovely photo! I never thought I'd see anything of the sort! My Susan looks a picture, doesn't she? And she looks even more blonde than I remember... And just look at Courtney – he's a really handsome young man, isn't he! He's tall, too! Now I find it easy to understand how she fell for him, and I can understand why he was the apple of his Dad's eye too!'

'There are some more for you to look at, Grandad... No more of the wedding, of course, but some more of Mum and Dad with me.'

Wilf looked at the photos, beginning with those which depicted Ruth as a baby sleeping in her pram and progressing through Ruth's teens until he came to another wedding group. 'Ha!' he said, 'This must be your wedding, Ruth!'

'Yes,' Ruth replied. 'So what do you think of your daughter in her forties?'

'In her forties? Oh gosh, she doesn't look that age, does she! But of course she must have been... When was this photo taken?'

'Well, Michael and I were married in February 1982 – so how old would that make Mum?'

'She must have been 43 at that time then! Well, well, she does look good, doesn't she! And look at Courtney too – he's the image of his Dad too, but not quite as dark. And don't they look happy! That's the thing that I was most worried about, you know – I was frightened that they would find life a real struggle...'

'I think there were times when it was a real struggle for them,' Ruth commented, 'but they got through it all right.'

'Thank God they did! And to be blessed with such a pretty daughter as you too...'

Ruth laughed. 'But having a pretty daughter is no guarantee of a happy life, Wilf! Look at you and Cissy…'

'Yes,' but I'm happier today than I have been for years – I wasn't even as happy as this when Forest won the European Cup!' Wilf said, with tears streaming down his face.

At length they decided it was time to call a halt to proceedings, and for Michael to drive Wilf home. As Ruth was about to say goodbye to her grandfather, however, she said, 'Now, Wilf, I've just realised that we haven't talked about Christmas – we'd like you to come and spend Christmas with us.'

'That would be nice,' Wilf agreed, 'but there's only one problem. I've already agreed to go out for Christmas Dinner.'

'Oh, where are you going?'

'Ernie invited me round to his place…'

'Ernie? You mean Courtney's Dad?'

'Yes.'

'Well, that's all right then, because the next thing I was going to do was ask you if you thought he'd like to come too!'

'I'm sure he'd be delighted, but the invitation's got to come from you, not me.'

'Well, yes, but I haven't even met him yet! Will you take me to meet him?'

'Yes, of course I will – when?'

'The sooner the better. Let's see… Tomorrow's Tuesday, and I've got to go to work tomorrow. I can't have two days off in succession! Oh no, to hell with it, this is more important than work! What about tomorrow morning?'

'That's okay with me... But I can't promise Ernie will be in.'

'Well, if he's not, we can leave him a note.'

'Okay.'

'And I'd better bring Emily with me of course... Shall I pick you up about ten o'clock?'

'Yes, that's fine for me. And bring some photos with you too.'

When Wilf went to bed that night he felt just like a little boy on Christmas Eve, waiting for Father Christmas to come: far too excited to sleep, he kept turning over and over in his mind the wonderful things that had happened that day – little short of miraculous, he thought. And among those happy thoughts were mingled regrets that Cissy had not lived to see this happy day. But, he reflected, Susan had hardly been blessed with good fortune either, for she too had not survived long enough to see Emily's happy face; just thinking of Emily's smile as she had said good night to him that evening was sufficient to make him break into a grin. A lot of things happened in life, he thought, some good and some bad, and the really important thing was not to allow the experience of unhappy moments to prevent you from appreciating the moments of great happiness when they came.

A Happy Christmas

He thought too of his friend Ernie, who had as little idea of what lay in store for him tomorrow as he himself had had the previous day; and he smiled again in anticipation of the pleasure which awaited Ernie as he learned one new unsuspected fact after another, to say nothing of the introduction into his life of blood relatives of whose existence he was as yet totally unaware. What's more, he felt a much closer bond with Ernie than before, and, as he drifted through that twilight zone which serves as a transition between being awake and being asleep, he felt as if he were flicking through the pages of a photograph album full of happy pictures; but with this difference – the events portrayed in this album had not yet taken place.

Then, all of a sudden, it seemed, it was morning and he was wide awake. He jumped out of bed with an energy and an enthusiasm which he had not experienced for many a year. He put the kettle on, gave Boots his breakfast and then made tea, which he drank while getting dressed. After that he took Boots out for his early morning walk; it was a dull morning, but he felt the sun shining in his heart. He looked at his watch: it was only eight o'clock, so still two hours before Ruth and Emily were due to arrive. He went back home, made toast and another pot of tea, had breakfast and then looked at his watch again: it was still not yet half past eight. He sat, thinking what he could possibly do to make the time pass more quickly… What would Cissy have done, he wondered? He jumped up, went into the kitchen, then returned to the living room carrying a duster. He dusted the dresser, the chairs, the television, the mantelpiece and all its trinkets – how on earth did Cissy manage to spend so much time dusting? By the time he had dusted everything in sight he was disappointed to find that no more than fifteen minutes had elapsed…

'Oh, I don't know, Boots,' he said to the dog. 'What can I do to make the time pass more quickly?'

Boots just sat and wagged his tail.

Wilf had a sudden thought. 'I know!' he said to Boots. 'Let's go for another walk!'

As usual Boots made no objection, and they went out together, but today, it seemed, Boots seemed to be trotting along with more purpose, Wilf thought. Or was it that he had more purpose himself?

'Good morning, Wilf! Hello, Boots!' he heard a woman say, her voice interrupting his thoughts. He looked up and saw it was Sheila.

'Hello, Sheila,' he said. 'I'm just taking Boots for a walk.'

'It looks more as if he's taking you,' she said. 'When I saw you walking towards me you looked as if you were in a different world…'

'I was,' he admitted.

'It looks as if Mrs Elliott brought your glasses then,' she observed.

'Mrs Elliott? Oh, yes, Ruth… Yes, she did – and you'll never guess what happened then!'

Wilf proceeded to tell her the story, and by the time he had told Sheila about his new granddaughter, his new grandson-in-law, his new great-granddaughter, to say nothing of a new great-grandchild apparently in the offing, she could not stop herself laughing.

'What did I say?' Wilf asked. 'Why are you laughing at me?'

'Oh, Wilf! I'm not laughing at you – I'm laughing for you! What wonderful, wonderful news! I'm laughing because I'm so happy for you! I've already told you that you were a born grandfather, haven't I! And I've watched you over the last few weeks bringing so much happiness into little kids' lives, and now it's flooding back into your life too! That's what happens – happiness is infectious! I've never seen you look so happy, and such a wonderful thing couldn't possibly happen to a nicer man!'

'Thank you, you're very kind,' replied Wilf. 'But I'm sorry, Sheila, I must get back home again, because Ruth and Emily are arriving at ten o'clock. Come on, Boots, we need to get a move on!'

With that, Wilf strode off as quickly as he could, with Boots's little legs working overtime in order to keep up. Just as they arrived home, Ruth's car drew up outside the house, and Emily came running up to him.

'Great-grandad!' she cried. 'Oh! What a beautiful little dog! What's his name?'

'His name is Boots. Boots, meet Emily. Emily, meet Boots...'

'Can I hold him please?'

'Yes, of course you can,' Wilf replied, handing the lead to Emily.

'Can I take him for a walk?'

'He's just had a long walk – he's probably ready for a rest now. And while Boots is having a rest, we've got to go and visit somebody…'

'Can I stay with Boots while you and Mummy go?'

'No,' Ruth answered before Wilf had time to react. 'Boots will still be there when we get back, don't worry!'

'Where are we going?'

'We're going to somebody else's house.'

'Whose house?'

'You'll find out when we get there! Now hop in! You too, Wilf!'

'I can't yet – we can't go until I've taken Boots inside!'

'Oh, I'm sorry, Boots! I was forgetting you!'

'Poor little Boots!' said Emily as Wilf took the dog inside, before coming out again and getting into the car alongside Ruth.

Two or three minutes later the car drew up outside Ernie's house in Burford Road. The three of them got out of the car, and Wilf rang the doorbell. Initially there was no answer, so Wilf rang again; this time they heard footsteps approaching, the door opened and Ernie appeared. At first Ernie saw only Ruth and Emily. 'Good morning,' he said politely. 'What can I do for you?'

'You can let us in, Ernie, it's only me – there's somebody I'd like you to meet,' said Wilf.

'Oh, it's you, Wilf, I'm sorry, I didn't see you there! Come in.'

He led them into a small sitting-room, invited them all to sit down and then offered them tea or coffee.

'No thanks, Ernie,' said Wilf. 'We've got too much to talk about for now, but later you might need something stronger than tea!'

Ernie looked puzzled, but proceeded to sit down next to Wilf, who held out a photograph for Ernie to take.

'Now then, Ernie, I've got something to show you. Is there anybody in this photo that you know?'

Ernie looked at Susan and Courtney's wedding photo and Wilf waited for him to react.

'Hey! That's my son Courtney!' he exclaimed all of a sudden. 'And that's your Susan too, isn't it ? Where on earth did you get this?'

'I'll tell you that in a minute,' said Wilf. 'After I've shown you this one...'

Wilf handed a second photo to Ernie, another wedding picture, but this time of Ruth and Michael's wedding. Ernie looked at it, looked at Wilf, then at Ruth, then at the photo again.

'This is this lady, isn't it?' he asked Wilf, indicating Ruth. 'It looks like a wedding photo...'

'Yes, it is, it's my wedding,' said Ruth, who had been dying to speak since they first entered the house. 'And the other couple, do you know who they are?'

Ernie's eyes moved back to the photograph he was holding. 'I don't know… Just a minute, can it be? Is that Susan and Courtney again?'

'Yes, it is – got it in one!' cried Wilf triumphantly. 'Now stand up, Ernie. You too, Ruth…'

They both did as they were told.

'Ernie,' said Wilf. 'Yes, Ernie, this is the bride in that photo, and… You may kiss the bride, because she's your granddaughter!'

'What did you say? What are you talking about?'

'I'm Ruth. I'm Courtney and Susan's daughter!' said Ruth. 'And if you don't want to kiss me, I jolly well want to kiss you! That's two new grandads in two days, grandads I didn't know I had! That must be some kind of record!' She kissed Ernie on the cheek and continued, 'But we haven't finished yet! This little girl is Emily, and if I'm your granddaughter, Emily must be your great-granddaughter!'

'What! This little cutie! I bet she's the Dancing Queen from the Abba song!' He made for Emily, swept her off her feet, and danced around the room with her, with Emily giggling all the time. 'I can't believe it!' he said, after setting her down again. 'Look at me!' he went on, 'and now look at her. How can I have a great-granddaughter as pretty as that?' He jumped to his feet again. 'Come on, young lady, let's have another dance!' And he whisked Emily off her feet again and danced around the room once more.

'Now then, Wilf,' Ernie said, once his dance had stopped and he had flopped, exhausted, into an armchair, 'I guess there's a lot to tell me – there's a lot I want to know, that's for sure!'

'Yes, there is,' Wilf assured him, 'and you'll hear the whole story before long. But there's one thing I'll tell you now which I'm sure is uppermost in your mind, as it was in mine, and that's about Susan and Courtney. Now I came to terms years ago with the fact that I was never going to see Susan again, and I know you reached the same conclusion about Courtney. All I want to tell you now is that none of that's changed, we'll never see either of them again – you'll hear the reason why when the little one isn't here – but what has changed is that, even though our kids are lost to us, *their* kids aren't, and neither are their kids' kids. And there's another bit of good news too – in a few months' time little Emily is going to have a little brother or sister…'

'Wow! That's great news!' cried Ernie, getting up and going over to Ruth. 'I was just going to ask this young lady if I could have the next dance, but perhaps in the light of what Wilf's just told me, perhaps we'd better not…'

'I think a little twirl wouldn't do much harm,' said Ruth laughing, and she proceeded to dance around the room with him just as Emily had done. 'It's lovely to see how happy you and Wilf are about this sudden extension to your family, but I want you to know that I'm tickled pink in exactly the same way you are!'

'But,' Ruth continued, 'I hate to break up this reunion party, but I really do have to go in to work this afternoon, so I'm afraid I've got to break it up. But I have a feeling that we've got some really good times together waiting just around the corner. Now listen, Ernie – Grandpa, Grandad – we're going to have to sort out what to call everybody, aren't we! Anyway, Ernie, we've already invited Wilf to come and have Christmas Dinner with us, but he said no…'

'He said no? He must be crazy! Why on earth did he say no?'

'Because he said he'd already accepted an invitation from you…'

'Oh well, I'll let him off that…'

'Only if you come as well – let's make it a real family Christmas!'

'Why not? I think that's a great idea, so yes, I accept your kind invitation – but I'm going to make one condition…'

'What's that?'

'I'll come to you on Christmas Day on condition that you all come here to me on Boxing Day for a Jamaican celebration…'

'That sounds wonderful – thank you!'

So Wilf, Ruth and Emily said their temporary farewells to Ernie, but not before Wilf and Ernie had rearranged their weekly drinking rendez-vous in the Carlton: they decided to meet that very evening instead, because Thursday seemed much too far away – after all, it was now Tuesday, and they both had a lot of celebrating to do!

A Happy Christmas

Later that evening Wilf arrived at the Carlton first, so he bought two light ales as usual, and went to sit at a little table in the corner where they always sat. Ernie arrived almost immediately; Wilf stood up to greet him with an embrace, rather than the Jamaican thumb-rubbing handshake which Ernie had taught him a few weeks earlier, but Ernie said anxiously, 'Be careful, Wilf! Let me put this down first!'

Wilf stood back while Ernie placed a plastic carrier bag reverently on the chair before accepting Wilf's hug. After their greeting Ernie resumed his seat, picked up the carrier bag again, and then he too sat down.

'Don't look so worried, man!' he said. 'And forget about drinking this rubbish, I've got something here that's much better than that!'

He looked around to ensure that no one was watching – especially the landlord – and then removed two small glasses from the carrier bag and placed them on the table alongside the two glasses of beer. Only when he was completely satisfied that nobody was watching him did he withdraw a bottle from the carrier bag, remove the stopper and pour a golden liquor into the two empty glasses. Then he replaced the bottle in the carrier bag and hid it carefully under the table.

'What's this?' asked Wilf.

'This is the nectar of the gods,' Ernie proclaimed. 'We have something big to celebrate, don't we, and this is the only thing for a self-respecting Jamaican to celebrate with!'

'Ah, is it rum?' Wilf enquired.

143

'It is rum, but I bet it's rum as you've never tasted it before. Look!' Ernie bent down, retrieved the bottle once more and showed it furtively to Wilf. Wilf glanced at the label and was just able to read, 'Appleton Estate 12 Year Old Jamaican Rum' before Ernie hastily concealed it under the table again. 'I was saving this for Christmas,' he said, 'but I think we'd both agree, Christmas has come a little early this year!'

'Yes, indeed it has!' Wilf agreed. 'Cheers!'

'No, a proper toast!' Ernie insisted. 'I want to drink to Courtney and Susan, and their family!'

'I'll drink to that!' replied Wilf, and so began a far longer drinking session than was their norm. For two hours they talked and drank; Wilf related to Ernie as much as he knew about Susan and Courtney, their life in London and their premature, tragic death, followed by the complicated chain of events which had led to his leaving his glasses at Ruth's house and the revelation that had ensued.

'This is all truly amazing,' said Ernie. 'All these new relatives in one go! Granddaughters, great-granddaughters, grandsons-in-law... So what relation does that make me to you, Wilf?'

'Don't ask me,' said Wilf, laughing. 'Some sort of cousins? I don't know...'

'What about brothers?' Ernie suggested. 'I'd settle for having you as a brother...'

'Yes, I'd go along with that! I always wanted a brother!'

'I bet you didn't think you'd end up with a black one though!' said Ernie. 'Say, I was going to say this earlier, but I didn't want to mention it with all the others there. Way back, when we first found out that Susan and Courtney were going out together, we were both worried about what their kids might turn out like, weren't we? You know, mixed race and all that… So now you've seen her, and the next generation as well, what do you reckon, eh?'

'I reckon we were daft, Ernie, that's what I reckon. You never know what the future holds anyway… But I didn't imagine that they'd have a daughter as gorgeous as Ruth…'

'Nor a granddaughter as beautiful as Emily!' Ernie added. 'Aren't we lucky!'

'I think that's worth raising a glass to!' Wilf suggested, and Ernie readily agreed.

At last they decided that it was time to call it a night, and walked out of the pub, rather more unsteadily than usual – leaving two glasses of light ale, undrunk, on the table.

In the seven shopping days which remained before Christmas, Wilf and Ernie had their work cut out, particularly in comparison with the previous year. Not only did they have to buy a Christmas present for each other, but Ernie had to do all the shopping necessary to be able to prepare his promised Jamaican banquet on Boxing Day. And then they each had to buy – for the first time in their lives – a present for their granddaughter Ruth, to say nothing of her husband Michael. In addition, Wilf felt the need to buy a special present for Sheila Hardcastle too, because if she had not advertised for a Father Christmas he and Ernie would have been spending a lonely Christmas again, just as they had the year before. It followed, Wilf thought, that Boots too deserved some extra special dog biscuits for compelling Wilf to stop and read the advertisement. And then of course there was Emily. Unbeknown to each other, they each bought her a big doll, the best they could find; to Wilf's and Ernie's mutual surprise and delight, there was one marked difference between the two dolls: the one bought by Ernie was white, and the one bought by Wilf was black.

On Christmas Day Michael came to pick up Wilf and Ernie in his car to take them to Victoria Crescent, for Ruth, naturally, was busily occupied in the kitchen. When they arrived, Emily came running to the door to greet them. 'Look!' she said excitedly. 'Father Christmas has been – and look what he's brought me!' She then offered her two new little girl dolls for them to inspect, and then added, 'The white one's called Susan – and the black one's called Courtney…'

Not for the last time that day the eyes of all the grown-ups filled with tears, even though their mouths were smiling. And in the circumstances, none of them thought it mattered in the slightest – nor was it even mentioned – that Courtney was a boy's name, not a girl's.

Michael came into the drawing-room at that precise moment carrying a tray bearing four glasses of champagne and a glass of lemonade; when each person was holding a glass he raised his and said, 'I think all of us will agree that this is already by far the happiest Christmas we've ever experienced, so this toast is more in recognition of what we can all see happening before our eyes, than a wish for something delightful to happen... A happy Christmas!'

'A happy Christmas!' said Ruth.
'A happy Christmas!' said Emily.
'A happy Christmas!' said Ernie.
'A happy Christmas!' said Wilf, smiling broadly, for he was, at last, a happy man.

THE END

Tony Whelpton

The Author

Although he is nearly 84, Tony Whelpton has written five novels in the last five years, *A Happy Christmas* being the second to be published this year.

He has been writing books for nearly forty years, but turned to fiction late in life, and has been so successful that he wishes he had started earlier! He is the author of thirty or so school and college text books – mostly in French – as well as two books on cricket and a history of the Cheltenham Bach Choir, of which he recently became Vice-President after retiring from singing at the age of 80.

Tony Whelpton

He was born in Hyson Green, Nottingham in January 1933, and was educated at St Mary's Junior School, High Pavement Grammar School, Goldsmiths College (University of London), Birkbeck College (University of London) and the University of Lille.

He taught French for four years each at Beckenham & Penge Grammar School and Lowestoft Grammar School, then moved into Higher Education, ultimately becoming Principal Lecturer in French at Trent Polytechnic (later Nottingham Trent University), where he spent seventeen years. For more than a quarter of a century he was a nationally known figure, being Chief Examiner in French at O and A Levels and also at GCSE.

He is also an experienced journalist and broadcaster: he produced and presented the first ever schools programme on UK local radio, a French programme on BBC Radio Nottingham for junior schools, called *Écoutez, les enfants!* He has sung at the BBC Proms, he came second in the European Final of the World French Spelling Championships in 1990, and appeared on *Mastermind* on BBC1 in 2009.

His first novel, *Before the Swallow Dares* (published 2012), concerns two old school friends who get together after a break of nearly fifty years, as a result of a chance meeting. One of them discovers that the other is married to a girl whom he loved at school, but who, to his utter devastation, disappeared without trace and never answered his letters.

His second novel, *The Heat of the Kitchen* (published 2013), takes us to Saint-Pierre-sur-Loup, a fictitious village in France, where the Mayor is wrestling with a common problem in the south of France: too much traffic for the town. His favoured solution succeeds in upsetting most of the inhabitants, and he finds himself in a fight for his political life.

Billy's War (published 2014) takes us back to Tony's home town in 1941, a year and a half after World War Two broke out, and begins with an air raid which he remembers well, although the district where he lived did not receive many of the bombs; but he has such vivid memories of the shrieking noise of falling bombs followed by explosions that he felt compelled to use that as his starting-point for *Billy's War*. But Tony is *not* Billy, his mother was not killed and his Dad was too old to be in the army, having served in the final stages of World War One and spending World War Two in the Home Guard – sometimes known as *Dad's Army*.

Billy's War was so successful, and the character of Billy so popular that Tony decided early on that a sequel was required: *There's No Pride In Prejudice* (2016) is the result. It has nothing to do with Jane Austen: the title comes from a statement made by Billy Frecknall in the book, expressing an idea which he adopts as his motto throughout his distinguished life. One romantic attachment after another makes him realise the widespread influence of prejudice throughout the world, and he decides to devote his life to fighting discrimination of every kind wherever it occurs.

Tony Whelpton

Tony's attitude to life is that it is there for living and he believes that getting old is not an excuse for sitting around doing nothing; one of his favourite quotations comes from the French cellist Paul Tortelier: 'Everybody should die young – but as late in life as possible'. Now you understand why Tony is still writing!

If you would like to know more, check out Tony's website at www.literarylounge.co.uk and follow him on Twitter (@SwallowDares) or like his Facebook page Tony Whelpton Novelist.

Even more importantly, if you have enjoyed reading this book, please take a few minutes to write a review on the Amazon website!